I0776212

Love, Lewes

D. J. GRIFFIN

ISBN Paperback: 979-8-9910963-0-0
ISBN Ebook: 979-8-9910963-1-7

Cover design by Jason Griffin
Sketches by Greer Maneval, ArtByGreer.com
Design and publishing assistance by The Happy Self-Publisher.

Book Lovers Press

For Mako...

Dream bigger

1

The conversation might have gone differently had I known I was talking to a ghost.

For a warm, late summer day he was overdressed: faded long-sleeved cream blouse, gray pants, and some type of wool vest. An odd combination, as though he'd selected random items from the local thrift. My first thought was that he might be homeless, except he had absolutely no odor. With my exceptional sense of smell, what should have been my first clue, I somehow dismissed.

He sat quietly with his hands resting on his legs, parked on my favorite bench in front of the Zwaanendael Museum. Damn. Was hoping to have it all to myself. His gray-streaked brown hair was long enough to be pulled back with a black tie of sorts and he made no indication that he'd noticed my approach. Studying his attire again, I thought he was wearing period clothing. Maybe a docent for the Lewes Historical Society?

I preferred this spot because it sat at just the right angle for a portrait of the museum. It was such a cool building with its steep, peaked roof, fancy brickwork, and red and white decorated shutters. Very narrow, yet very tall, it looked as if it had been plucked from the streets of Amsterdam. The museum sits at the intersection of Savannah Road and Kings Highway, and I could hear the occasional car drive by, but I paid them no mind.

Sketch pad in hand, I studied my seatmate one last time, decided he looked harmless enough, and sat at the far end. Putting my watercolors between us, I spritzed them with a small atomizer and began dabbing ochre on the outline I'd already drawn.

Despite having to share my space, I couldn't wait to continue to work on this piece. Sketching and painting took me to my happy place—a place where time had no meaning. I'd get totally absorbed studying and capturing the details of a building. I had less than two hours before I had to be behind the bar, but until then, I could lose myself watching the color flow onto the paper. This wasn't something I created to be sold or graded. It was just for me.

Once my hands were happily engaged, I let my imagination soar, wandering through the rich history and mysteries of this nearly-400-year-old town. Not the typical musings of a twenty something woman, I know, but much more satisfying than my love life or lack thereof. Don't even get me started.

"What does Zwaanendael mean?" I could hear Livia's voice in my head, which always made me smile. That five-foot capsule of historical passion and unbridled energy who owned the bar grilled everyone. Employees and patrons alike. We loved it.

Zwaanendael, the original moniker of my beloved hometown, meant "Valley of the Swans." It was the name the Dutch gave to Lewes, Delaware in 1631.

My boss was an avid, rabid Lewes historian. If you worked at her bar, it was hard not to be infected by her enthusiasm.

Every Thursday was local History Trivia night, and you could barely get in the door. Because of her, I knew the English eventually ousted the Dutch and that the Delaware colonies were later given to William Penn. Penn thankfully changed the name of the town to Lewes, 'cause that old Z word was a bitch to spell.

Between the art and the history, my favorite bench often became a magical transport to another place and time. Somewhere away from the home of a twenty-eight-year-old single bartender who didn't have a clue what to do with the rest of her life.

My benchmate sat perfectly still throughout my arrival and assemblage of materials. He seemed so deep in thought; I didn't even say hello. But once I got going, I could feel his eyes on me. Glancing sideways, but still engrossed in what I was doing, I said, "Didn't your mother teach you it's rude to stare?"

"I beg your pardon?"

He said this so softly I almost missed it. A British accent? If so, it was ever so slight. Must have been in the States for a while.

I turned so I could see his face better and looked into icy blue eyes, the palest I'd ever seen. His brow was creased, but he didn't look puzzled or offended. Instead, his face registered more disbelief than anything else.

"Sorry," I said. "I'm hungover and being rude. Good morning." I gave him a tiny smile and glanced back at my work. My shoulder length hair kept falling around my face, so I quickly pony'd it with the scrunchie on my wrist.

"You can see me?" A note of surprise filled his voice.

"Yeah. That's what happens when you buy an Invisibility Cloak off eBay. They just don't work as well." Snarkasm. My specialty. Refocusing again on my painting, I worked to get more color on the paper before my paints dried.

He threw his head back and laughed from his toes.

Thinking he got my Harry Potter reference, I grinned. I love it when people think I'm funny.

I heard him whisper, "she can see me," then suddenly, he was gone. Not like, he jumped up from the bench and ran away, but like freakin' POOF. Not there. I stood and did a 360 and then wondered how much I'd really drunk last night. Guess the eBay cloaks work after all.

Zwaanendael Museum

2

Most days you'll find me behind the bar at Grace O'Malley's, a pub named after a famous female pirate. Though several pirates have visited the Delaware shores, Grace did not. Instead, she stayed close to home, terrorizing the waters of her beloved Ireland. At one time, Grace commanded an entire fleet, giving the English Navy a run for their money. Wildly successful, she died owning four castles of her own. Our fearless leader, Livia Kelly, a woman of Irish descent herself, said she appreciated women in history who had kicked some ass.

The pub was housed on the first floor of a boutique hotel at Second and Market in the downtown Historic District. The corner entrance opens into a large space with stools and counters lining the windows. Patrons facing Second Street can watch the parade of visitors in and out of King's Ice Cream or Biblion Books. Those facing Market have a view of the numerous white headstones of St. Peter's cemetery, possibly the oldest in Delaware. My favorite grave belongs to Captain Henry McCracken, who requested his anchor be buried with him. It's a great way to get restless kids out the door to find the grave where the fluke of an anchor now sticks out of the ground.

As I stood behind the mahogany bar cutting limes for the night, I was glad I'd made the time to sketch. Despite the odd encounter, art was my mental sanctuary. I'd taken a few classes over the years but kept it just for fun and just for me.

Thinking about the man on the bench, it seemed odd that he had no smell. None. Not sweat, not soap, not cologne. Nothing. With my 'smart' nose, I could differentiate between Dove, Caress, Dial, and Irish Spring, and men's colognes like Dior Sauvage or Paco Rabanne. If I couldn't guess the brand, I knew when the main ingredient was rose, violet, or lily for women, or bergamot, musk, or patchouli for men. It was a fun trick for a bartender to have until some idiot felt he needed to be on top of me so I could get a whiff of his Axe body spray. Eww.

I wore the standard black dress shirt and black pants that was our uniform but added a tiny pin to my collar that said 1631. The year Lewes was founded. Most of the time, I wore either small silver hoops or pearl stud earrings, but rarely bracelets or necklaces to work. What I did love and always wore were rings, tiny silver bands with different patterns. I would stack two or three on several fingers. I had dozens of them. Truth is, I like my long slender fingers. Of course, this meant long size ten feet as well. Those I wasn't as fond of.

At three p.m., the tavern was quiet, but I knew by four we'd be jammin'. The town of Lewes sits where the Delaware Bay meets the Atlantic Ocean so in addition to the period charm of an historic seaside village with lovely boutiques, restaurants, and quaint gray shingled B&Bs, we have miles of beautiful beaches. Which translates to lots and lots of tourists.

The door swung open—I could tell without looking by the way the light changed in the room. I hoped it wasn't a large group so I could finish setting up and restocking what the night crew had demolished.

"Hey, girl."

I loved the sound of that voice. The sexy, late-night-radio timber of the one, the only, Paris Savannah Harrison. His momma had named him after the City of Light and he was my best friend.

"Hey, yourself. What are you doing here this early? No weddings to plan?" I paused from polishing stemware to make his favorite afternoon cocktail.

Paris was the most sought-after event planner at the Delaware beaches. He also managed an exceptionally competent team, so most likely they were working away even as he graced my presence. He parked his six-foot four ebony self on the stool in front of me and sat his designer shoulder bag on the one beside it.

"Do NOT, I repeat, do NOT get me started. Rich people have more money than sense, that's all I have to say." Paris took a monogrammed handkerchief from his linen pants pocket and patted his glistening head. We were having a warm September which meant the tourists were still here in abundance. Good for business, but after a wickedly busy August, I was ready for a break.

Sliding a Queen's Cosmo across the bar, I noted his crisp white shirt accented with tiny beach ball cufflinks encrusted in colored rhinestones. His attire was perfect despite the heat.

"Do tell," I begged, catching a whiff of Bleu De Chanel, his new favorite fragrance.

Paris frowned at my forehead. "Listen Cara Delevingne, you let those things get any more out of control and we'll have a full-blown Frida Kahlo on our hands. I can fix that you know." He reached for his man purse.

"Stop. I like them just the way they are." I laughed, covering my face. Paris preferred thin, perfectly shaped brows, while mine were anything but. I liked a strong brow, and I loved actress Cara Delevingne's look. I also wished I had her blue eyes as opposed to my almond shaped brown ones. "Tell me about the rich people. What now?"

Paris examined his long, manicured fingers currently sporting pale blue polish. "You know the family who owns the Broadkill Inn, right?"

"Sure do." Many a night we'd escorted the youngest son out of the restaurant because he felt entitled to do whatever the heck he wanted. Pain in my ass.

"Well, the duchess, as I call her, is paying a pretty penny to get her award-winning French Poodle impregnated by the latest winner of the Westminster Dog Show. But she wants them to get married first." Paris whipped out a red Chinese fan covered in dragons and started waving it around his head.

"Wait, what? The dogs are getting hitched, and she wants you to plan the wedding? That is just ... too precious." I shot my hand in the air. "Can I bartend? Pretty please?"

"Of course. You know you're my girl. But can you imagine? And, if that isn't enough, she wants the wedding to have a *theme*. I quoted her twice what I thought about charging, and she did not bat an eye." Paris shook his head. "It's all good. Momma needs a new pair of shoes." Paris slid his Chanel sunglasses down his nose, raised a perfectly plucked brow, and we burst out laughing.

Twice a month, Paris performed at the Pines, a popular restaurant in Rehoboth Beach that hosted a drag brunch every Sunday. His stage name was Lady Sue Nami, and he was, in my humble opinion, the very best. He spent a fortune on his costumes, wigs, and shoes, so of course he was more than happy to take the doggy gig. Besides having the best drag accoutrement, Paris was also a fabulous performer. In sky high heels and oversized wigs, he became an imposing seven feet tall. He was also amazingly limber, able to do a chorus line kick as well as a split. And the same wild creativity that made him the ultimate event planner went into each and every performance.

We chatted more about the doggy nuptials. Paris said they were expecting a hundred guests. That meant two bartenders, so I decided I would ask Skate from Heirloom, another restaurant in town, to join me. He was also a member of the Paris fan club, but more importantly, worked hard and was responsible, so he was always my first pick for sidekick.

Paris had chosen an Alice in Wonderland theme, with the poodle dressed as Alice. This had delighted the duchess to no end. Both two legged and four legged guests would be served from an assortment of vintage china, including teacups and saucers.

By four o'clock, O'Malley's was more than half full and I knew it would be a busy night. Paris gave me a little finger wave as he left, waving his phone at me which meant we'd talk later.

Throughout the night, my mind wandered back to Paris and the upcoming Alice in Wonderland doggy nuptials. I loved bartending his events. Not just for the money, although Paris paid well, but for the spectacle. His reputation was well deserved. Getting in on the spirit of things, I would concoct one or two special drinks for each soiree. Since I already had a Mad Hatter cocktail on the menu at Grace O'Malley's, I decided to go with a White Rabbit and the Red Queen.

Knowing I'd spend the evening creating two new drinks in my mind, testing the recipes and getting the opinions of my favorite locals, made me happy. Still, I was getting restless behind the bar, though I had no clue what to do next. The only thing I knew for sure was that I wanted nothing more to do with medicine. Ever.

3

My full name is Genevieve Alexander Stewart. Everyone calls me "Vie" (like Vee), except my mother when she's pissed. Then it's my full given name being shouted at the top of her lungs with her five-foot two inch frame. My middle name is my father's first name. Had I been a boy, I would have been Alexander Dorchester Stewart II. How my brother got away with just Finn, is beyond me.

Thankfully, I took after dad in the height department, falling just two inches short of his six feet. We both have dark hair and brown eyes, while Finn was my mother's clone: fair and blonde with grey-green eyes.

My father had been a beloved and well-respected surgeon at Sussex General, the largest hospital in lower Delaware. Before I turned ten, I was already announcing to the world that I too, would become a doctor. I couldn't wait to follow in his shoes.

By high school I had determined my specialty would be pediatrics, until I mentioned this to my father, who told me, "It's one of the hardest units I've ever worked on."

"Why? I would think working with kids would be the best place of all," I remembered asking. I was all of sixteen.

"If they're on the mend and doing well, it's like babysitting, which isn't so bad until you're running after them down the hall because they're using an IV pole as a skateboard."

This made me laugh.

"But if they're really sick, it's heartbreaking. You want every child to have the opportunity to grow up and feel like they can do anything, but sadly some of them will never get that chance." He told me that during his pediatric rotation in a large city hospital, a little girl had come in with burns on both hands because a drugged-out babysitter had put them on the burner of a stove. Even though this had happened before I was born, my father was still very emotional talking about it. He said we are often unaware of the horror and the cruelty that can, and does, exist in our own backyard. As pleased as he was that I was interested in medicine, he wanted me to understand that beyond my idealistic vision of being the hero who saved lives, I'd be exposed to a reality I hadn't known.

Though my choice of specialties became less certain, I was undaunted in my pursuit of following in my dad's footsteps. There would be four years of undergrad before the four years in medical school, so I would have time to consider my options.

Two years into college, I got a call from Dr. Fellows, an orthopedic surgeon and close friend of Dad's. They often sailed together. A young woman had been in a car accident and died in the ambulance on the way to the hospital. Her husband had arrived shortly after and was inconsolable. He left, returning an hour later. Readmitted into the patient area of the emergency room, he pulled out a gun, yelled to the staff that they had taken everything from him, shot two hospital personnel, and then himself. My father, who had never met the man or his wife, died instantly. I was twenty-two.

My mother immediately went to bed, and for the most part, stayed there for six months. Finn, who was sixteen, began to skip classes and hang with a crowd known for drug use. I left college, came home and stayed home, trying to mend the broken pieces of my family.

Finn eventually found his way back to water and surfed or skim boarded as much as he could. Two years later, he left Lewes, working his way around the world, doing odd jobs, following the waves. From time to time, I'd get a text saying he was ok, that he missed me, but wasn't ready to come home. The more information I pressed for, the less I got. Eventually, he responded more frequently to my texts, and would share his location and some tidbits about his life. At present, he was in Hawaii, learning to scuba dive. He had apologized belatedly for leaving mom in my lap, but I confessed back to him that had anyone else been there to care for her, I'm not sure I would have stuck around either.

My mom eventually crawled back to life and found a new man. It was a relief to see the return of the loving spitfire who raised me. Despite her independent spirit, Mom was a woman who enjoyed being pampered, and I was grateful it was no longer on my shoulders. Like Finn, she had no desire to stay in Lewes following my father's death and moved to Sarasota, Florida with her new husband.

When did I grieve?

Not sure I ever did. I went on autopilot, telling myself there'd be time for that later. I just kept imagining my father on my shoulder, counting on me to take care of everyone in his absence.

4

I'd arrived early to work and sat at the counter facing Market Street overlooking St Peter's and the cemetery. Sipping my coffee, I glanced through an art magazine, checking out an article on alcohol paints, something I wasn't familiar with. An ad for Blackwing pencils grabbed my attention—I'd been given a set that I really liked. I glanced at my phone to check the time when movement in the cemetery caught my eye.

It was the mystery man who had vanished from the bench. He really did exist. Wandering slowly through the gravestones, he paused thoughtfully beside a few, as if to read the marker. Others he touched reverently, speaking to himself. He was dressed in the same clothing I'd seen earlier, which seemed none the worse for wear.

Before I knew it, I was out the door, crossing the street, and bounding up the few brick steps to the cemetery. Coming up beside him, I sensed such sorrow in his demeanor; I couldn't think of anything to say. With head bowed and shoulders drooped, he seemed far away, lost in his thoughts.

"Hello again," I said, almost in a whisper. Something in me wanted to comfort him, but I stopped myself from touching his shoulder. Again, no smell. So odd.

I'd startled him and he twitched before turning to face me. Straightening up considerably, a slow lightening and brightening spread across his countenance. How do I describe this? Like more life flowed through him. The tension and sadness in his face dissipated, and he smiled almost shyly at me.

"It's you," he said at last, looking happier by the minute.

Yes, I wanted to say, but found myself dumbstruck. Why in the world was I eager for another encounter with this complete stranger?

He looked like he had all the time in the world, a never-ending well of patience. What was that like? I couldn't imagine as I often tried to multi my multi-tasking. There was an ease about him and a calmness I had no reference for.

"I'm Vie, short for Genevieve," I said at last. I started to put my hand out, then thought better of it, being on the tail end of a pandemic. "We met the other day. Well, sort of, in front of the Zwaanendael Museum. I was painting—"

"I remember." His smile revealed a left dimple, his eyes bright.

Normally, I'm Chatty Cathy, according to Livia, who grew up playing with her older sister's doll of that name that spoke when you pulled a cord. At the bar I can talk to anyone, no cord required. But now I was still struggling with what possessed me to run out of the pub. He reminded me of someone, but who? With the lines around his eyes and mouth, and the gray in his hair, he looked to be in his fifties.

"I'm Robert Henry Edward Talbot. My mother had a fondness for English kings." He chuckled. "Call me Henry." He put one foot back, an arm behind his back, bent his knee slightly, and gave a little bow, almost as if he were starting a dance from a period film.

Not wanting to offend, I covered my mouth to hide my grin. "Do you live here?"

"Oh, yes." His shoulders slumped again.

Wrong question, I thought. Feeling awkward, I started to back away. "Well, I just wanted to say hello and introduce myself, and I'm late for work, so um...see ya." I walked away briskly, still questioning my motives. Rather than go directly into Grace O'Malley's, in his line of site, I walked down Second Street, cut through the alley between the toy store and the bank, and came in through the rear entrance of the pub.

I immediately went behind the bar, mindlessly checking stock for the evening. Remembering his formal bow, or whatever that was, I smiled. Not able to help myself, I once again wiped the already clean counters at the windows to see if Henry was still there. He stood in front of the covered porch at the church entrance, studying it as though he was curious as to how it was built, looking underneath, and touching the posts. I hadn't thought to ask what he did. Maybe he built things. Carpenter? Contractor?

George, one of my regulars, came in, so I reluctantly tore myself away from stalker mode. Slipping behind the bar, I poured his Glenfiddich neat. He was in his mid-fifties with an amazing head of salt and pepper hair and a huge mustache which gave him the nickname, the Walrus. We had several nicknames for our regulars to help the newer staff keep everyone straight. There was the Diva, who had to tweak everything she ordered, including a glass of water (rocks glass, two lemons, no ice), or the house burger (with the lettuce, tomato, and a slice of cheese on a side plate, bun extra toasted and the whole thing cut in quarters). We also had to be careful not to actually call them by our cheat names. The Walrus was well-liked and had great stories from being a retired pilot. Not an airline pilot, as you might think, but a river pilot, a longtime occupation of many in our town, keeping the larger boats off the reefs.

With our Irish moniker, patrons came in expecting the Celtic vibe and corresponding food, so we offered the standards like burgers, fish and chips, and, of course, the requisite shepherd's pie to keep the masses from rebelling. But Livia loathed being put in a box and kept the rest of the menu both delightful and surprising. We had unexpected things like cauliflower tacos, which were totally amazeballs, and mouth-watering muffalettas, the classic sandwich of New Orleans.

Without being asked, I handed the Walrus the tiny blue menu for locals, which we kept under the bar. This was my doing, and I was rather proud of it. Many restaurants had off-menu options—unadvertised dishes that were written nowhere. These could be ordered provided the ingredients were available, like the Butterbeer Frappuccino at Starbucks.

We actually printed ours weekly, along with certain specials for which we had limited ingredients. Tourists might inquire about the smaller menu printed in blue, and we'd hand them one as well. As expected, everyone delighted in feeling like an insider. Livia loved her locals. Loved spoiling them and making them feel integral to the success of Grace O'Malley's.

"Hey, George," I said. "We have lentil soup tonight, and it's amazing. Would go really well with a ham and cheese toastie." I winked and made him laugh.

"You know me well, don't ya. Sounds perfect." George tipped his whiskey in my direction, then slid the secret menu back to me. The sounds of Aerosmith favored by the kitchen crew, changed to The Beatles' "Let it Be," letting me know that Livia was now somewhere on the premises.

A couple came in and sat next to George. With all the empty seats this early in the day, it gave me a warm fuzzy feeling seeing strangers gravitate to one another.

"Can I get you something to drink?" I asked.

The man was engrossed in his phone, but looked up once he heard my voice. "What do you have on tap?" His dark curly hair was tipped with blonde, and his hazel eyes were rimmed with thick, dark lashes.

Oh, my freakin' God—he was the spitting image of Logan, my ex. I realized I'd inhaled and then forgot to breathe. Shit. "Um, Sam Adams, Blue Moon, Guinness—"

He put his hand up. "Stop right there." He gave me a big grin which I felt in my knees. "I'll have a Guinness." Turning to the woman beside him, he said, "Sorry babe, I jumped right in. What do you want?"

The pale, slender woman studied me intently, as though my frantic thoughts were running across my forehead like a tickertape.

"We have a wine and cocktail list, if you'd like to see," I mumbled, looking down as though the list was lying on the floor.

"What's a ham toastie?" she asked, bringing her long blonde tresses forward; fluffing them a bit, like she was about to take a selfie. An herbal scent wafted from her hair, but I pegged Chloe's signature jasmine scent as her fragrance.

Grateful to focus on Blondie while I regrouped, I took a deep breath. "A traditional Irish sandwich we make in a panini press, with shredded cheddar, Irish ketchup, and ham." Anticipating her next question, I continued. "Irish ketchup is a little sweeter than ours, chunky, kinda like a salsa." Being nervous, I kept going. "In Ireland they call it relish." *Stop talking, Stewart. Just. Freakin'. Stop.*

Logan's doppelganger jumped in again. "That sounds amazing, I'll take one of those. I glanced at your menu online but didn't see that."

I avoided his eyes while I put down paper coasters and the rolled-up emerald cloth napkins containing silverware. "It's on our secret menu," I mumbled. "Let me get your Guinness." Thankfully he wasn't wearing Logan's signature Calvin Klein, or that would have done me right in. I wiped my now sweaty hands on my pants, then shook them. Holy Mother of God. What had I done in a previous life to deserve this? I was instantly transported to being that bride on the beach where the groom doesn't show. I shook my head as emotions rolled through me like waves before a storm. The anger and heartache I had buried hard and deep for the past twelve months broiled just beneath the surface.

As I tipped the glass against the tap, Wick, the other bartender came up beside me.

"Good god, Vie, is that Logan's twin brother?" He nodded towards the bar.

I stopped mid pull as there was already too much head on the beer which happens when you're not paying attention. "Jesus, right? What the hell?" I looked skyward. "Not funny."

"Want me to take 'em?" Wick studied my face with concern.

I shook my head. "Nah. I'm cool. It's all good." Liar, liar, pants on fire.

Wick took the glass gently from my hand and nudged me towards the kitchen. The night was a blur after that.

*   *   *

A year before, I'd been standing in the soft warm sand of Lewes Beach, expecting to be a married woman by sunset. Paris had done a beautiful job of keeping it simple, with the concession that he'd be allowed to go full blown Studio 54, Mardi Gras or whatever, for the reception. Folding white chairs formed a semi-circle with a path up the middle, lined with hundreds of seashells and twinkling lights. Around the area where we were to be joined in holy matrimony were columns of fabric, lit from within, with the bay as our backdrop.

My fiancé, Logan, had texted that he was running late, so I came out of the beach house we'd rented for the occasion to wait with my guests. Despite the delay, I remember being ridiculously happy to be a barefoot bride in the most beautiful gown you can imagine; an off-the-shoulder fitted lace top with a tea-length tulle skirt covered in tiny beads and sequins that fluttered in the breeze. My hair was pulled back in a soft chignon, with tendrils around my face, and I wore a tiny pearl and diamond choker that my dad had bought me for my high school graduation. I was surrounded by the twenty people I loved the most and considered my family. Though I couldn't get Mom to leave Florida, my brother Finn had flown in from Australia to be by my side.

Thirty minutes after we were supposed to start, Logan texted to say he wasn't coming —he needed time to go find himself. In shock, I let the phone slip from my hand into the sand. Finn retrieved it, read the message, muttered something to Paris, then hurled the bearer of bad news into the dark water. Then he gently guided me back inside while Paris broke the news to my incredulous friends.

My fiancé, who was on track to become partner at his father's law firm, had decided being an attorney was no longer his heart's desire.

Apparently, neither was I.

Grace O'Malley's

5

The day after seeing Logan's double, my sketch pad and I found ourselves on the canal, not far from Grace O'Malley's. Docked in front of me was a large, red ship, otherwise known as a lightship, or a floating lighthouse. This one was over one hundred feet long, with the word Overfalls on its side in big white letters. She'd been built in 1938 with an electric lantern that could be seen for twelve miles, another obscure fun fact floating around in my head thankyouverymuch, Livia Trivia. It was the perfect subject for my next drawing. Anything to get my mind off the night before.

Paris had texted to see where I was, appearing in my line of vision shortly thereafter. Shading my eyes, I looked up to see him in an iridescent three-piece suit that almost glowed in the sun.

"Ground control to Major Tom." I giggled. "What time does your rocket launch?"

"Oh, we're hilarious this morning. I'll have you know this is the perfect outfit for Disco Divine, the theme of tonight's soiree." He pirouetted for the full effect.

"Wait, what? I'm off today, why didn't you call?" I frowned at the towering beacon of light.

"Oh, honey, don't hate me—thank me. These are not fun people. They vetted their own staff for the event. I even had to subject my minions to a screening that would rival a Top-Secret clearance. But they pay very, VERY, well." He grinned.

I relaxed. "Ew. Ok. Thanks, I guess."

Paris sat beside me. "What is wrong, my pouty princess?"

I paused, tapping my pencil on the edge of my sketch board. "Logan's twin waltzed into the bar yesterday. It was weird. And painful. And just …"

Paris laid my supplies gently in his lap, slid over, wrapped his long arm around me, and kissed the top of my head. "He didn't deserve you and I'm glad he's gone."

It had taken months to recover any semblance of self-esteem I had left. Logan had phoned many times, but I didn't answer. Then he wrote letter after letter saying how he really didn't know who he was, how much he had disappointed his father, that he didn't want to disappoint me, and blah, blah, blah. He'd left Lewes the night of the wedding and was living somewhere in Maine, working at a ski resort. Go figure. I leaned against Paris' shoulder and sighed. "Do you think he found himself?" I wrote quotation marks in the air as I said, 'found himself.'

"Doubtful." Paris scooched back a bit so he could see my face. "And that reception would have rocked our world, honey." He smiled.

"What does that mean, find yourself? Why would I care if he didn't want to be an attorney? I'm a bartender for crying out loud." We'd had this same conversation over and over and over and over.

"I do hope you're getting some. Doesn't sound like it." Paris adjusted his silver rimmed Ray Bans and watched a very attractive man walk past our bench. "Dibs."

"You're married, beeatch. And you just said *I* needed to get laid." I shook my head and feigned offense, then we both laughed. "Speaking of that, where in the world is Rafael?"

Like Waldo, Paris' husband could be anywhere in the world. Rafael located homes and investment properties for extremely wealthy clients, who would put him on their private plane, jetting him off to Portugal, Paris or Dubai on a moment's notice.

"Croatia, I believe."

The sun dipped behind a cloud, and I tossed my sketchpad into the grass. "This is not happening." Trying to draw when I was in a weird space never worked. I was still feeling icky about seeing my ex/not ex last night. Like when you throw up repeatedly and there's nothing left. Physically and emotionally depleted from reliving my shame, I decided it was time to change the channel. "Hey, did I tell you I've been chasing a homeless man around town?"

Paris took off his sunglasses and stared at me. "If you're that desperate I can show you how Tinder works."

Giving Paris the dirtiest look I could muster, I said, "Look. He's my father's age and I don't really know if he's homeless, or not. Last I saw him was in the cemetery. He just looked really sad. So I introduced myself and found out he has four names. All kings. Robert Henry Edward Talbot. But there's no one by the name of Talbot buried there, because I searched..." Still rattling incomplete sentences, my mind drifted off, wondering where Henry was and why he was orbiting my world. Behind us the courts were full of pickleball players, and I could hear them whacking the balls and goading each other on.

Paris' phone buzzed and he had to go. "Do you want the name of my therapist? Or my stash of CBD gummies? Either way, I'm worried about you." He squeezed my arm and started to walk away, then stopped. "Seriously. You, ok?"

I nodded and shooed him away.

Despite our snarky banter, I loved Paris. He was a gift that came to me in 2017, a year after my dad died. I was at the wedding of a bride and groom who were bar regulars, and they'd hired Paris as their planner. He'd hired two bartenders, but one had had an allergic reaction to the flowers and was taken to the ER. This I found out later, as it was all done very discreetly. The remaining bartender struggled to keep up. She was good at mixing, but not fast. I was both. We knew each other on sight, so when I offered to help, she said absolutely. Within minutes the line was gone, and with her permission, I made a few tweaks in the setup to make life easier.

"Vie, you're a lifesaver. I can't thank you enough."

For the life of me, I couldn't remember her name. "Oh my god, you're so welcome."

Just then Paris strolled by and introduced himself. "Well, hello there, Wonder Woman." He extended a well-manicured hand. "Thank you for coming to our rescue."

Paris with a presence. Wowza. The man was six-foot six, or so I thought, not knowing he always wore at least a two-inch heel. Slightly muscular, but not overly so. He was dressed in a stunning charcoal gray suit, with black satin lapels. The material had a slight shimmer to it, which immediately read 'fun' in my book. His skin was a rich mahogany color, and his eyes were so dark it was hard to tell where the pupil ended, and the iris began. Shaved head, and diamond rings on several fingers.

"Genevieve Stewart, but my friends call me Vie. Happy to help."

Paris studied me for a moment. "See me before you leave, would ya, darlin'?" And off he went.

The young woman beside me said, "He'll take good care of you. Always does. His team adores him. They call themselves 'the Paris Posse.'"

Later that evening, as the reception wound down, Paris found me. "You weren't going to leave without saying goodbye?" he purred, handing me an envelope.

"You know, with that voice, you could always do radio, or voiceovers," I suggested.

"But then no one could see all this fabulousness." He laughed, sweeping his hands from his head to his toes.

I cracked up and pushed the envelope back at him. "Happy to help. I'm usually at Grace O'Malley's, but I can give you my number if you ever need backup."

"Then let me buy you a drink." His long arm swept the room. "My crew has this covered."

"Um, sure. Sounds great."

The wedding and reception were at the Inn at Canal Square, a lovely spot right on the water, so we agreed to meet at Kindle, barely a block away, in fifteen minutes.

When I arrived, Paris was parked at one end of the bar, sipping a Cosmo. He had on rhinestone encrusted readers and was studying the late-night menu. "I'm starved. Can never eat at those things. And I can't believe I had to send a bartender to the ER. Good Lord." He fanned himself with the menu.

"Hey, Brody," I said. "I'll have an Italian Greyhound." The bartenders and servers all knew each other. Small downtown.

"Hey, Vie. No problem." Brody glanced at Paris, then turned to make my drink.

"An *Italian* Greyhound? Ain't you fancy." Paris laughed.

"Ruby red grapefruit vodka, limoncello, grapefruit juice, and prosecco," I recited. "It is divine, and you are going to wish you had one." Brody served my drink along with a small stainless shaker on the side. I asked for a shot glass and poured Paris a sample.

"Well, well. I just found my new drink." He slid his empty martini glass back to Brody. "Sir, if you would be so kind as to mix me an *Italian* Greyhound, I would be most appreciative. And the bill is mine no matter what this young lady has to say."

Sipping my cocktail, I studied Paris. I'm terrible at guessing someone's age, but I'd put him at least ten years my senior, so... early 30s.

Paris' phone buzzed. He studied the screen, and I could see his shoulders relax. "Oh, thank god, my bartender is fine. They sent him home with some Benadryl."

We made small talk around that for a moment, then Paris' eyes widened. "Not to be personal, but I've heard your name. I just remembered reading about your father. I'm so sorry."

My dad's death had been in the news forever. The beach towns of lower, slower Delaware rarely experienced violent crime, and he had been a well-loved figure.

I nodded, not sure what to say.

Paris continued, "My eighteen-year-old brother was shot and killed when I was sixteen. You never get over it."

It was our bonding moment. That my beloved father met such a horrific end was still a tangled mess in my mind. So much anger. So much grief. Yet Paris, too, had experienced the nightmare and the horror of a similar catastrophic event. Had known the rage and loss and feelings of helplessness that followed. It was all I could do to not fall on him and sob. Like being from Mars and finding a fellow Martian after feeling a lifetime alone.

6

Over the years I'd become Paris' bartender of choice depending on my schedule at O'Malley's. Better yet, we'd become family. We had the same love of sarcasm, movies, and an obsession with fabulous food. Our small towns meant the world to us, his Rehoboth and my Lewes, and we tended not to share gossip, except with each other. The same violence that had bonded us, aged us, and we fell easily into deeper conversations about life, death and love.

That day near the Lightship Overfalls, Paris had asked if I was ok. I wasn't. My bleak thoughts slithered back to being an abandoned bride. Heartbreaking and shameful all at once. I thought Logan had been loving and kind, but how well do we know anyone?

My thoughts took me from Logan's father to my own, and my mind dipped to the saddest thoughts possible, tucked in deep, dark crevasses that held my most profound grief. I had grown up assuming I would be a doctor, which I knew would have made my dad immensely proud. Maybe we'd even have had a practice together. And one day he'd walk me down the aisle to a husband who would most likely embody all of dad's best traits. The things that made me adore him. Always present. Very thoughtful. The best kind of listener. Never took anything for granted.

Looking around my tiny digs, I thought a second about going back to bed but decided I needed a change of scenery before I could no longer climb out of this pit of despair. I grabbed my art gear, threw it in my trusty backpack, and steered my bike towards the beach.

Even though it was almost October, the sand was warm. I sat on one of the many white benches, looking over the bay. How could I fault Logan for 'going to find himself' when I struggled with the same dilemma? But where in the manual did it say you abandon the people you love while figuring it out? Then again, what if I'd finished medical school, went to work at Sussex General and then decided it wasn't for me? Could I have disappointed my *own* father? Or would I have escaped as well?

At work later that day I was still noodling hard on a future career. The music changed to Carole King and Livia came in wearing her typical black jeans, a black and white houndstooth blazer, and a red T-shirt from her vast collection. From a distance the graphic looked like the standard movie poster of Godzilla amongst tall buildings, but when she got close, I saw Godzilla had been replaced with a giant squirrel. Hilarious.

Despite her small stature, Livia's presence filled the room. Her long reddish blond hair, now with streaks of silver, hung in a braid on her back, and her readers rested near the tip of her button nose. A smattering of freckles helped belie her age of fifty-five. The same age my father would have been.

"I think we're short on limes and there were none in this morning's delivery. Can you run across to Agave and see if they'll spot us some 'til tomorrow?" Livia stopped scribbling on her clipboard and studied my face. "You're miles away, Stewart. What's on your mind?"

At work, she called me by my last name. At family gatherings, I was Genevieve or Vie. Livia had been to my parents' house on numerous occasions. She felt like the younger sister my father never had. Their banter had been loving, playful, and at times unexpected. Most people had seemed intimidated by my father, who was well known and respected, but Livia gave him grief at any and every opportunity. A much better cook, she would nudge him away from the grill with a, "move aside rookie; let the pros show you how it's done."

"Just trying to figure out what I wanna be when I grow up." I started checking stock to see what else I'd need for the evening. While most pubs and restaurants had one large streetside window, because of the corner, we had two. I loved how much light there was throughout the afternoon and how it changed as the sun began to set. There were two rows of stained glass above both of the large windows, and the colors they cast around the room were an artist's delight.

"California Dreamin" by The Mamas & The Papas played in the background and Livia sang along as she worked. She loved pop music from the 60s and 70s, but not the edgier rock like Aerosmith and AC/DC, favored by the kitchen staff. She paused in her inventory and studied my face. "You thinking of going back to school?" She raised an eyebrow.

"I haven't a clue." Was that wishful thinking on her part? Should I go back to school? I glanced out the window to see if Henry was in the cemetery. Any distraction would do.

"Well, you're great here. Organized, responsible, confident—you're definitely someone I could see managing or owning a bar. And I've seen you in the kitchen. You've got some chops there too."

With that, Livia strode towards the back, mumbling about another item on the order, and I was once again alone with my thoughts. As I moved chairs off the tables, I made sure it had been carefully swept and that the tops were really clean, since I hadn't closed the night before. I was the person who always went behind everyone else, making sure everything was perfect. Vie the responsible. I was glad we kept nothing on the tables like wire holders with salt and pepper, or containers of various sweeteners. Too many times while dining out, I'd see those items slid over to a bored child, who proceeded to destroy it at their discretion.

Kids. Wanted 'em. Would that ever happen? Maybe. Still time. Lemme figure me out first. I was a great bartender and loved helping in the kitchen whenever they were short staffed. Would I want to own a restaurant? Become a chef? Teach art? History? Was there any vestige of a medical dream left in my bones? Everything I tried on I shed instantly, like a dress that looked great on the hanger, just not on. As though making a choice would only lead to regrets.

7

I'd finished the sketch of the lightship days ago, and now wandered the little park belonging to the Lewes Historical Society, looking for my next subject. The Shipcarpenter Street Campus, as it was known, had nine historic buildings: homes, a country store, blacksmith shop, doctor's office and a school building. Options for days.

I decided on the doctor's office with the Greek columns. Because of Livia, I also knew it had been a tailor's shop, was built around 1836, and was the only example of Greek Revival architecture in all of Lewes. It was late Thursday morning, which meant I had a few hours before the pub. The leaves were turning on the trees around me, so there was color both above and below where they carpeted the ground. I shuffled through them on purpose, kicking them this way and that, remembering jumping into piles as a child. The bench that gave me the best angle was in full sun, so though the air was crisp, I wasn't cold. Closing my eyes, I inhaled and exhaled deeply, enjoying the smell of the grass and trees and the sun on my face.

"Hello again, Miss Vie."

The voice startled me, and I sat up to find Henry standing several feet away, still dressed in the same clothing. "Oh hey, Henry." Now that I'd seen this a third time, it looked like a period costume. Had I been wrong about him? Was he a docent after all, and just wore this all the time? Wandering around, staying in character while answering questions? Or was this his clothing of choice? An image of Finn wearing his favorite Spiderman costume to school weeks on end made me smile.

"Might I join you?" He gestured to the bench.

I was caught up in how perfectly he fit in this historical setting, with its buildings from the 1700 and 1800s. Could I put him in my sketch? Maybe. I'd never tried drawing people.

Henry put his hands behind his back and looked away, as though embarrassed or … something.

I realized I hadn't responded. "Um, sure." I slid my stuff over to give him room. "Are you like, a reenactor or a docent, or…" I paused, wondering if he were neither, would he be offended? His brow wrinkled and I bit my lower lip, thinking this had been the wrong way to start the conversation.

"You are referring to my clothing?" He looked down at his attire, then back at me.

Nodding, since words were apparently unavailable, my mind scrambled as to where else to steer the conversation. Then a wash of calm came over me which I just realized had happened each time I was in his presence. Was this what drew me to him? It was as if all was right with the world. Something I hadn't felt since my father died. Suddenly I was so happy, I almost cried.

Studying my face, Henry looked puzzled. "Are you alright?"

Again, I nodded, too afraid if I spoke, tears would come. Dad had been the rudder, our center, and nothing had ever been the same. What was I feeling now, a sense of peacefulness? No, not the right word. Ease? Nope. *Anchored*. That was it. My tether had broken upon my father's death, and in Henry's presence, it reconnected. It was both glorious and heartbreaking.

Henry put his hand towards my shoulder, then drew it back. "Should I go? I'm terribly sorry if I've disturbed you."

"No," I blurted. "Please. Stay." I looked away for a moment, trying to regain my equilibrium. What a gift. Thank you, Henry.

We sat in silence for several minutes, and it never felt awkward. I nestled happily in the memory of what it had felt like before dad died. My father had been a grounded and happy man. Content in his choice of career, his passions like sailing, and his family. Our house had been a safe harbor where I knew I was loved, no matter what.

Henry sat back, hands clasped across his middle, like he'd eaten a fine meal. He occasionally turned his head to watch the leaves swirl around on the ground, but otherwise was still. Hardly anyone was in the square, though a few people walked by. They nodded or said hello to me, totally ignoring Henry. Weird, considering he'd dressed the part.

Shifting to sit sideways, he turned and asked, "Miss Vie, are you a believer in the woo?"

"The what?" I laughed.

"I think you young people call it woo-woo, or ..." he paused. "Something of that nature?"

"Oh totally," I said. "I love watching the Long Island Medium, she's terrific. And you can't live in Lewes and not hear ghost stories. There's too much history here." Seriously. I loved this shit. I turned around and pointed to the Burton-Ingram house. "Everyone thinks that one's haunted." I knew it was one of several stops on the paranormal tours. When I turned back to look at Henry, he had the most impish look on his face, like I was about to be pranked.

"What?" I asked, waiting for the punchline. Just then a couple walked past, nodded and said hello to me and didn't even look at Henry. "Seriously? That is just rude. They totally ignored you."

"They can't see me."

All the hairs stood up on my arm, and a chill ran through my center. He'd said this so softly, I almost missed it. "What?" I knew we'd been talking about ghosts, but I didn't think this was funny.

Henry stood and paced in front of the bench, clasping and unclasping his hands. Then he paused and gave me a look of such sadness mixed with something I couldn't place.

"I don't mean to frighten you, but you're the first person who can see me in over a hundred years."

8

My mouth opened, but nothing came out. A woman jogged by, nodding my way. Henry waved his arms wildly as he was almost in her path, but she never paused.

Was this a trick? An illusion? Was the woman so focused she didn't see him? Maybe she thought he was crazy and was just ignoring him?

Dammit. After basking in the knowledge of what drew me to him, I now had to decide if Henry was delusional. Or off his meds. Or what, I didn't know.

"I've frightened you. I'm terribly sorry." Henry kept his distance.

"No. Not exactly. Well kind of." I hugged my sketchbook to my chest like a shield. *Crap. Please don't be crazy. Be a docent. Be a historian.* I'd been happy to see him and now I wasn't sure.

"Please, forgive me. It's just … it's been so long. I'd forgotten how much I—" He struggled with some emotion, then closed his eyes and shook his head slowly. "Again, my apologies. Goodbye, Miss Vie." He gave a little bow and walked quietly away; shoulders slumped.

Now I felt bad. Whatever this was, I didn't want to hurt his feelings. The finality of his goodbye jolted me, and I realized I wasn't ready to be rid of him despite my concerns. "Henry, wait."

He did not stop.

Shit. "Henry!" I scrambled off the bench and ran after him. Reaching out to touch his shoulder as I came up behind, my hand had the sensation of moving through cold Jell-O. I gasped.

He turned just then, mouthed, 'I'm so sorry' then faded away. Suddenly there was nothing there. Nothing at all.

My knees buckled and I ended up on the ground, shaking. What the hell? Putting my hand on my chest, I tried to calm myself, but found it hard to take deep breaths.

"Are you alright, dear?" A tiny, elderly woman stood over me, her face full of concern.

"Did you see the man in period clothing?" *Please say yes. Please.*

She shook her head but looked around as though she might have missed something. "I'm sorry, I did not. All I saw was you running and yelling Harry and then you crumpled. I'd offer to help you get up, but I'm not very strong." She looked chagrined at that last confession.

Oh great. Now *I* look like the crazy person. "I'm ok," I said, getting up from the ground, brushing leaf debris off myself. "Thought I saw someone I knew." I reached out to pat her on the shoulder, thought better of it and shuddered. "Thank you, though. I'm fine."

Not.

Doctor's Office

9

In the days that followed I scrubbed my teeny apartment above the carriage house from top to bottom until everything gleamed. In the bathroom, the chrome fixtures shone, and the porcelain sink and tub were the whitest they'd ever been and everything smelled bleachy clean. Using an old head on my electric toothbrush, I attacked the caulk between the black and white floor tiles till it looked brand spanking new.

My mind could not make sense of what had happened. The manic maid mode I now embraced was my effort to think of anything else. The studio space held a full-size bed tucked into a large dormer under a skylight, a comfy love seat, miniature kitchen with a vintage fridge, and a small table with two upholstered chairs. A voracious reader, I'd lined every available wall with bookshelves, even parking my bed in front of one. Continuing my housekeeping frenzy, I removed every book and dusted it, even wiping the shelves themselves. Every windowsill, every pane of glass.

At night when I couldn't sleep, I'd haul my laptop in bed and search for hours for everything paranormal. History of ghosts, Lewes ghosts, famous ghosts. There was a new show called *Ghosts*, but the commercials for it looked silly and I couldn't do it. Of course, I say that, yet I found myself watching *Ghostbusters*, the movie, and pondering ectoplasm, the ghost substance the movie refers to.

My hand had touched something otherworldly. Every time I thought about it, I looked at my fingers expecting some type of evidence that the whole thing had really happened. Contact with Henry had not left any residue, yet there had been contact. Wouldn't my hand have passed through a real ghost? *A real ghost— do you hear yourself?* Or a spirit. Ghost or spirit? What's the difference? Why don't we throw in the idea of an alien for good measure. *Shit, Stewart. You're losing it.* I reminded myself he never said he was a ghost, just that no one had seen him in over a hundred years. That meant at least 1922. But he wasn't dressed like he came from that era, his apparel was more from the late 1700s, early 1800s. Trust me, I'd researched that as well.

I hadn't told Paris or anyone what had happened. After my father's death I had learned to compartmentalize, so at the pub, I was all business. Grace O'Malley's had never been cleaner or more organized. If Livia noticed, she didn't say anything. She knew I was pondering what to do with my life, so I hoped she would attribute it to that. Every day I watched the cemetery for signs of Henry, but nothing. Even if I saw him, what would I say? *Hey Henry, I've decided to be friends with a ghost, let's chat.* Good grief.

The love of Paris' life had returned from Croatia, so I hadn't seen him in days. When he finally made an appearance, he immediately knew something was up. Lost in thought, I missed his arrival, so by the time I did notice, he was already seated and tapping his bright white nails on the mahogany counter.

"My Queen's Cosmo, wherefore art thou?" he trilled.

"Oh, hey. Be right with you." In short order I slid the requested cocktail across the glossy bar top. "How's Rafael? How was Croatia?" I asked, wiping imaginary spots, avoiding his direct gaze.

Paris frowned at me. "How are *you*, is the question? You've barely responded to my texts, but far worse, have yet to comment on my ensemble." He raised his arms like the letter 'Y' in the dance for the YMCA song. With big blocks of white and primary colors outlined in black, his tailored suit resembled a Mondrian painting.

Normally, I'd have a witty comeback, but after so many sleepless nights of paranormal Googling, I had nothing. I held up my finger. "Gimme a minute to grab some more cranberry from the back." I scurried off to the kitchen.

By the time I returned, the bar was full. I busied myself everywhere but in front of Paris. When I slid him his second cocktail of the evening, he grabbed my wrist.

"I know you close at nine because it's a Wednesday, which means you'll be out by ten. I will be waiting. I will drive you home. We will talk." His eyes bored through me.

Nodding, I scampered off again.

It was great when the bar was busy because time flew— although I wasn't ready for it to go as fast as it did. What the hell would I tell Paris? He'd think I was nuts.

Right around ten, I locked the back door and saw the white Porsche sitting there with Paris inside.

"Hey." I climbed into the low front leather seat, admiring the immaculate interior. Paris loved his car and it still looked and smelled like it was brand new.

"Hey, yourself, Genevieve Stewart. What is going on?" His voice softened and he pivoted to look at me. "You know you can tell me anything. Is it work? Did Logan's twin shake you up? Talk to me." He laid his hand on my arm.

Oh, god, where to start? "Can we chat at my place? I'm ready for a glass of wine."

Nodding, he started the car and we drove in silence, parking in the driveway minutes later.

I stared at the huge, turn of the century house in the front of the property, took a deep breath then headed back to the carriage house above which was my beloved studio. Then I unlocked the windowed door and headed up the stairs.

"Girrrrl, I forget how teensy your library—I mean your apartment—is. Cute, though. Needs a little zhuzhing." Paris grabbed some wine glasses and splayed himself on my loveseat.

I opened a bottle of red and pulled one of the upholstered kitchen chairs over. He poured, we chinked, and I let out a huge sigh. "I met someone."

He sat up straight and leaned forward over the miniature red wagon with glass on top that served as my coffee table. "Do tell."

"Not what you think. Not romantic." I shook my head.

"Oh, no. Is this the homeless guy? Never mind. Keep going." Paris sipped his wine and studied me.

"As weird as this sounds, Henry—not Homeless" —I waved my glass at Paris— "makes me feel grounded. I haven't felt that way since my dad died, and it's almost—" I took a deep breath as I felt my voice waver. "Magical."

"Well, that's saying something." He stood and removed his Mondrian suit jacket, folding it carefully before laying it over the back of the loveseat.

"Yeah. Just one problem. He isn't real." I blurted my revelation, then stood and started pacing.

Paris blinked several times and said nothing. Just sat with concern on his face.

I mean, what did I expect him to say? *I* wouldn't know what to say. "Paris... I think he's a ghost." Then I sank onto the floor in front of the coffee table and stared up at my best friend.

"Oh, girl. What the hell. Really? No. Don't answer that. I know you and if you tell me it's a ghost, I believe you. We are in Lewes, after all. My mama saw spirits all the time and I was grateful NOT to inherit that particular trait." He shuddered.

"Right? But I touched him, and my hand didn't go through air, it was more like, um, Jell-O." I shook my hands at the memory of it.

"Oh. My. God. Ok, wait. I need deee-tails. Start at the very beginning and do NOT leave anything out." Paris refilled his glass and sat back into the cushions as I gave him the story of Henry.

He interrupted me often. At any point could you see through him? No. Did I ever feel afraid or threatened? No. Ok, maybe a little nervous when I thought Henry was delusional. Could I have been mistaken about the Jell-O? Oh hell no.

"Why do you think you're the first person to see him in all that time?"

"No freakin' clue," I mumbled through a mouthful of brie and crackers. The more we talked, the hungrier I got. Ella Fitzgerald sang softly in the background while Paris and I theorized my ghostly encounter until both of us were yawning so much it was comical.

"Girl, I need my beauty rest." He waved his hand around his face. "All this fabulousness does not come easily." Paris laughed and got ready to go. "Not that I'm going to sleep tonight thinking about ghosts and shit."

Sitting on the floor, leaning against the sofa, I finished my last glass of wine. It felt good that someone knew. Better yet, someone believed.

10

Weeks went by with no further sign of Henry. I found myself more sad than relieved. I had experienced something other worldly. Disturbing, yet kinda cool at the same time. While there had been moments of questioning my sanity, I now fully believed that I had made contact with the paranormal. Paris was also a believer, which was a bonus.

There must have been a dozen shows on television with investigators exploring haunted buildings, like abandoned prisons or former mental hospitals, but I couldn't watch them. Henry hadn't felt threatening to me in any way. It was just weird to have an experience for which I had no frame of reference.

Why was I the first person in a hundred years? If movies were to be believed, maybe we connected in order to help each other. Maybe something I said or did would help him crossover. Could I reach out to my father through Henry? Was he here to help me figure out the rest of my life?

Round and round my thoughts swirled until eventually I made peace with it. I had no compulsion to tell anyone else, and

I embraced that it had happened. It was a gift from the universe and it made me happy thinking about it.

And I wanted more.

Winters were mild in Lewes; sometimes we didn't get snow at all, and it seemed like it was going to be that kind of winter, judging by fall. The first week of November and the weather was still sixty degrees and sunny. I'd ridden my bike to the beach for my Tuesday morning yoga class. It still felt good to put my toes in the sand. The eight of us did our sun salutations, and down dogs and before I knew it, we were finished just as I caught sight of the ferry heading back to Cape May.

Heading back to my bike, I saw a lone figure sitting on one of the white benches. Even far away, I knew it was Henry. My heart began to race, and I stopped to have a quick conversation with myself. You don't have to engage. *But I want to.* We really don't know this man at all. *But who gets to talk to a ghost? It's a gift.* But—*Stop. We're doing this.*

I marched over to the bench. "Hello, Henry."

He looked at me and smiled but said nothing. Something about him seemed utterly defeated.

Sitting at the opposite end, I studied him. Same clothing he'd always worn, but now I realized it was all handmade—the way the wooden buttons were sewn on his wool vest, the hems on the sleeves of his blouse. I say blouse because the sleeves were rather full down to his wrist. There the fabric was gathered, then draped over the tops of his hands.

The band holding his hair was a leather tie. I again noticed the gray in his temples. While he was clean shaven, it wasn't the close, perfect one you see today. His hands were tanned and a bit rough, like someone used to manual labor. They were dry as well. I knew I had hand cream in my shoulder bag, which I offered freely to my friends all the time. Thinking about doing that to Henry made me giggle.

He looked over at me, frowning.

"I was just thinking of offering you my hand cream." I nodded at his hands. "But I don't know how that would work exactly."

He shook his head. "I'm not sure why you can see me. I've been trying to figure it out." He returned his gaze to the water.

I looked out at the bay. The water was especially calm and I remembered coming here with my dad. "I love this beach. My dad and I came here to learn to paddleboard."

He shifted so he faced me. "Paddleboard?"

Seagulls flew over our heads and some parked in the sand facing into the wind. Feeling lighthearted after yoga, and genuinely happy to be in Henry's presence, I jumped up and drew a full-size outline of a paddleboard in the sand. "It's a board about this big that you can stand on and paddle." Stepping into my drawing, I mimicked the motion of stroking the water.

He nodded as if he understood. "And why do you do this?"

I smiled. "For me it's therapeutic. Easy. Relaxing. That sort of thing." When I thought about it, we had so many leisure activities: paddleboarding, kayaking, surfing, skimboarding. Was leisure a strange concept to someone from the colonial era? I imagined it was. Part of me wanted to ask, yet something held me back, wanting him to lead the conversation. Henry stared at the drawing and was quiet.

It came to mind after our last meeting that if people saw me, they'd think I was talking to myself, so I purposely put in my earbuds, as if I were on a call. Too many people knew me from the pub, and I didn't want a rumor about crazy Vie talking to herself. Small town after all.

"Is that different from the one you sit on?" Henry leaned an elbow on the back of the bench.

"Yup. That's a kayak. There are several kinds. Some are sit-on-tops, and some you sit down inside, like a canoe."

"Yes. The long skinny boats. I remember those."

"Yes." Curiosity got the best of me. "Henry, are you a ghost?"

He stiffened. "Perhaps. Maybe. I'm not sure. Whatever this is, whatever I am, I don't want to frighten you. Please don't feel you have to talk to me." He turned his face away.

The feeling of calm swept over me, and I inhaled deeply wanting to breathe in every bit of it. Best of all, it once again transported me to memories of my father. Coming home for Christmas break after the first semester, totally exasperated with calculus. Dad was empathetic, told me funny stories from his time at college, and made the seas calm again. "I can't explain it Henry, but I feel grounded when I'm in your presence. This" —I gestured between us— "is how I felt around my father before he died, and it's a gift to experience it again."

"Really?" Henry looked surprised then pleased. "Well, that's something." He glanced at the water, smiling this time. Then he said, "I'm sorry for the loss of your father."

I nodded then closed my eyes, leaning my head back, letting the sun wash over me. I wasn't afraid, I was excited.

The possibilities of what I could learn from Henry in terms of history, made me giddy.

"Miss Vie, should I suddenly disappear..." He paused, brow creased. "Please do not be offended. I'm not always..." He looked down at his body. "Solid." Henry put his head in his hands a moment, then looked back at me. "I don't understand it."

While this was intriguing to me, I could imagine it would be exasperating, even frightening to him.

"Henry, when were you born? Did you live in Lewes all of your life? I thought I heard an English accent." Questions stacked in my brain like a line of dominoes. It was all I could do not to machine gun them right outta my mouth, I was so eager.

"Born seventeen seventy-three in England. Came here at nineteen and worked as a carpenter's apprentice."

1773? "Henry, that would make you two hundred forty-nine years old!" Oh. My. God. "And someone else saw you one hundred years ago, which would be around nineteen twenty-two... was that also in Lewes? And when do you think you—" *died*, I wanted to say, but that seemed rather rude. "Um, became a spirit?"

Henry held up a hand as though to stop me. "Miss Vie—"

"Just Vie, please," I said. "How—"

He shook his head. " I cannot address you in that manner. Respectfully." He bowed slightly.

"Ok, but—"

Again, the hand. He was smiling; this time the dimple made an appearance. "I feel it only fair that you provide information, as well."

"Tit for tat. Fair enough. Fire away." I sat back, arms folded. So ready for this. Couldn't wait, expecting to try to explain smart phones, credit cards, televisions.

"I would love to hear the history of your family and how you came to Lewes," he said. Then his face fell, he dimmed a moment, and turned to me with a look of desperation. "But first, will you help me find my family?"

11

Find his family? Find where they were buried? I wasn't sure what he meant. "I'd be happy to help. What is it you want to know?" There was so much pain in his face.

"I'm afraid I don't know exactly how or when I died. My wife was pregnant with our third child. And my sons..." He put his hand over his mouth as if to conceal his grief. "I'm not sure what happened to any of them after my passing."

"Oh, Henry." Empathy surged through me. The emotion in his voice made my throat tight. How could he not know? How many years had he searched for answers? Not just how they died, but more importantly, how they lived. Fearful he would vanish before giving me more details on what he did remember, I suggested we make a plan as to when and where we'd meet again.

Henry began pacing in the sand, which was interesting in that he left no footsteps. "Miss Vie, I'm afraid I have no concept of time. It is both a blessing and a curse."

I pondered that. How bizarre. And challenging. My mind raced with options. We couldn't reconvene at the beach since the weather was unpredictable. Which made planning an outdoor rendezvous a no-go. "St. Peter's cemetery, where we met the second time …" I was still staring at the sand at his feet.

"Yes." He clasped and unclasped his hands.

"I work across the street at Grace O'Malley's, the pub. The only thing I can think of is that I'll watch for you among the stones. If I see you, I'll take a break and we can duck into the back of the church and talk for a few minutes. How does that sound?"

"A break?" Henry asked.

Another foreign concept to my ancient friend. "I can stop working for fifteen or twenty minutes. Some people use it to smoke a cigarette, make a phone call—"

"This is acceptable to your employer?"

"Henry, trust me. It's fine. There will be another bartender to take care of the customers in my absence. It's a common practice." The sun went behind the clouds, and I hugged myself and rubbed my arms to keep warm. Did Henry feel cold? I wondered.

Nodding, he put his hand to his chest. "My deepest gratitude. You will be doing me a great service. I—" Then he was gone.

The hairs on the back of my neck stood and I shivered. I would *never* get used to that.

*   *   *

Back home I showered the sand away and lotioned the dry winter off my body. Holding the tube of Grapefruit Blossom, my favorite scent, I smiled, remembering the thought of offering it to Henry. Sitting close he looked real. Solid. It was amazing to me. When he was in that form there was nothing that suggested he was anything but a living, breathing, human being—unlike the reports of ghosts who appeared as everything from a white orb in a photo to a shadow at the end of a room.

I had so many questions. Could he see other ghosts? Who was the last person to see him? Could he move through walls? Then funnier ones. If I took a selfie, would he be in the photo? I laughed.

But the biggest question was, why me? Why could I see him. There had to be a reason.

But my questions could wait. The thought of his not knowing what had happened to his wife and sons was devastating. That he needed someone else to find his family. As painful as my father's death had been, I couldn't imagine not knowing how he died or where he was buried. Hopefully Henry's relatives were in a church cemetery, as there were so many unmarked graves in and around Lewes from the past 400 years.

Grabbing my laptop, I sat at my kitchen table and went to findagrave.com to see what info there was on Robert Henry Edward Talbot, born 1773. Date of death? Unknown. Guessing him to be forty-five at least, I put in a range of 1815-1820. No hits. Then I eliminated his two middle names and changed his date of birth to within five years of 1773. No hits. Then just his last name and approximate dates. Nothing.

Damn. If he wasn't buried in a marked grave, it was doubtful that his family was either. If they'd owned a farm, most likely they'd have a family cemetery.

Arrrrgh. I had so few details to work with. Shoving my laptop aside, I picked up my phone and went to the Notes app to make a list of questions. I needed to double check Henry's full name. I wanted to be sure there were no weird spellings. Then verify his date of birth and hopefully at least the year of his death. His wife's full name, maiden name and date of birth. I assumed that's who he most wanted to find, especially since she was pregnant. It pained me he never got to see his last child. The emotion that bubbled up surprised me. How could you live, not knowing what had happened to your children?

12

Normally I worked Mondays at the Pub, but Wick had asked for some extra shifts, so that freed me up to bartend for a Paris event.

This was a 50th birthday party for a woman who was a huge Star Wars fan. She was dressing as Princess Leia. While not a rabid fan, I had seen most of the Star Wars movies and enjoyed them while Paris had not. Though a quick study, he was hilariously out of his element. As I got ready to go, I found myself laughing, remembering the conversation we'd had when he first agreed to the gig.

"Who the hell is Princess Layla?" Paris had asked. He'd stopped to chat with Livia at the front door, so by the time he got to his seat, I had his favorite cocktail ready and waiting. He tipped the glass in my direction. "Bless you, my child."

"New event I take it?" I polished stemware while we talked. It was the start of shift, and the bar was fairly empty. Despite our large, lovely windows, the winter sun was so muted, I had all the lights on.

Paris nodded. "Star Wars theme. The birthday girl is dressing as the Princess. She's turning fifty and just loves that movie." He rolled his eyes. That night he'd been dressed head to toe in a deep cobalt blue suit, monochromatic with matching shirt.

I laughed. "Movies." I emphasized the 's'. "There's many of them." I rattled off words like Jedi, the Force, Darth Vader and Wookie, while James Taylor played in the background.

"Stop. Please, stop. You know I do don't *Star Wars, Star Tracks* or any of that superhero shit." Paris took the bar napkin from under his cocktail and blotted his upper lip. "Makes me sweat just to think about it. This is why I refuse to do children's parties."

"It's Star Trek, not Tracks, and Princess Leia, not Layla. You're too funny."

The evening of the soiree, I drove to Rehoboth Beach in my red Jeep, a car that spent most of its life in the garage below my apartment. Usually I walked or biked everywhere; one of the great joys of living in downtown Lewes. But the beach town of Rehoboth was five miles south, and it was cold out. The event was being held at the Sandbar; a venue located on the top floor of a hotel that sat right on the Boardwalk.

Unlike Lewes, which was located on a protected part of the Delaware Bay, Rehoboth Beach sat directly on the Atlantic Ocean. It was still light when I arrived, and the eighth-floor views were spectacular. From one end to the other it was a one hundred eighty degree view of nothing but sand and water, water everywhere. Endless waves lapping in from the horizon. I sighed happily. Living here never got old.

Several of the servers had arrived early. Some wore the white armor of stormtroopers, others in desert garb like the Jawa, or in the style of those in the Rebellion. Two selfie backdrops flanked the room. One was the interior of a spaceship, the Millennium Falcon; the other was a desert landscape showing two suns, a scene from the planet Tatooine. A band was warming up in the corner. Their sound resembled the band playing in the Mos Eisley cantina, a dive bar full of aliens, featured in the film. All of this was explained to me in excruciating detail by Leonard, a *Star Wars* fan on Paris' staff.

On the center table was the birthday cake; a miniature version of R2D2, a beloved pint-sized robot that helps Princess Leia.

Paris & Co had hired local actors to play some of the main characters in full costume, entertain the guests, and to pose for photo ops throughout the evening. I was sure the seven-foot furry Wookie, and the handsome man playing Han Solo would be very popular.

While Han certainly looked the part, he was decidedly not as charming as he thought he was. As I was setting up the bar, I overheard his ridiculous pick-up lines on the female staff. Unfortunately, I became his next target. "Is it hot in here, or is it just you?" Han asked, leaning over my pristine bar. "You look a lot like my next girlfriend." He grinned.

Rolling my eyes I said, "Read the room, Dude. You're embarrassing yourself."

Paris stepped behind the lackluster lothario and cleared his throat. Han slid off the bar and practically stood at attention. "Oh, hello sir, I was just getting some water."

Crossing his arms, Paris looked down on Han. With his black platform boots, he stood around six-foot ten. "If you want to get paid for this evening, and rather generously, you will cease hitting on guests or staff. Is that clear? If not, feel free to exit the building."

"Totally clear. Yes, sir, completely Mr. Paris, sir. Sorry." And Han slunk away.

Putting my hand on my chest, I gave a little bow. "Thank you, Mr. Paris, sir, for rescuing me." Then I started laughing and could not stop.

From the neck down, my beloved Paris was dressed as Darth Vader, the villain of the *Star Wars* films. It was obviously a professional rental, with the mechanical looking chest plate, black top, black pants and long black cape. In the movies, however, Darth wore a helmet/mask that covered his entire head which Paris couldn't do while running the event. So, for reasons unknown, he'd decided to top his bald pate with a black sequined beret.

The tears were rolling down my face at this point. "Oh Paris, who ARE you? Darth Gayder?"

He put his hands on his hips. "Ha ha. Next time I'll let Han Don Juan have his way with you. How's that?" And with a hmph, he swirled his long cape and stomped away.

Skate, the bartender from Heirloom and my help for the evening, had just returned with a box of stemware. "Ok. That, was hilarious."

I wiped my tears and we got to work.

An hour into the soiree, a man wearing a chef's jacket approached the bar. "Might I have a glass of bourbon. I'm putting the final touches on my bourbon caramel spice cake, and we just ran out in the kitchen."

"Sure. No problem." I poured the requested spirit into a large glass and was about to hand it over when Paris came back.

"Hey, Chef." Paris laid a hand on his arm. "The lobster stuffed mushrooms are divine. You absolutely know your way around a kitchen." He grinned. It was the first time he'd worked directly with this particular chef and I knew he'd been looking forward to it.

Their conversation gave me a chance to study Chef Bourbon. Standing next to Paris, I put him at about six two. His black hair was long and wavy, just brushing the top of his collar, and his eyes were dark brown with the most ridiculous lashes. With golden skin, he looked Mediterranean, or Spanish. Hard to tell. Either way—gorgeous.

Chef smiled. "Thank you, Paris. I love what I do. If will you excuse me, I need to get back." He nodded to me and mouthed thank you, as he took the bourbon.

Both Paris and I watched him walk away until he disappeared into the crowd.

"Dibs," I said.

"Oh, yes, girlfriend. And"—Paris looked at me, raising one of his perfectly plucked brows— "he's single."

Once the guests began to arrive, I was too busy to watch for Chef Bourbon, although from time to time I'd see him across the room, surrounded by women. While I didn't get a chance to sample much of the food, what I did have: the crab, pancetta and gruyere palmiers, and the spinach and onion fritters with mango chutney, was exquisite.

I had created two specialty drinks for the evening. The Dark Side, which used Kahlua as the base. And the R2D2, after the beloved robot made of white and blue metal, for which I used blue curacao, a liqueur made from the peel of the Laraha citrus fruit.

The evening whizzed by with everyone dancing, drinking, and eating. Paris gave good party, and Princess Leia was visibly pleased. Things wound down just after midnight. I was occupied behind the bar, getting everything back in place that had been there on our arrival, sending the glassware to the kitchen, packing up the decorative items, Paris' party napkins, and the various bottles of alcohol, ready for return, when a deep voice said, "Thanks again."

Chef Bourbon stood before me, smelling of coffee, vanilla and other hints of deliciousness.

Good grief, Stewart, pull it together before you start drooling.

"Nicholas Kosta, but my friends call me Niko." He reached a hand across the bar. His hand was strong and warm, and he gripped mine just long enough to make my toes tingle.

"Vie. Short for Genevieve."

"I liked the Dark Side, what's in it?" Niko had maybe two days of beard growth, nicely trimmed, and his dark brown eyes had flecks of caramel.

"Trade secret. I'd tell you, but then ..." I shrugged.

"You'd have to kill me, I know." He laughed. It was a good laugh, from the heart.

"Not necessarily." I crossed my arms. "I might just demand a recipe of yours."

"Oh, I see." He stroked his chin. "Dabble in the culinary arts, do we?"

"Some." I nodded. "What was in the fritters? I tasted carrot, spinach, and onion... and maybe some chiles?"

"Very good. They're called *bhajias*, and yes... you nailed the ingredients." He nodded.

Skate returned from carrying the glassware to the kitchen.

"What's next, Vie?" he asked, sizing up my chef.

"I'll let you finish up." Niko laid a card on the bar. "Call me sometime. We can trade recipes, perhaps?"

"Maybe." I tapped his card on the bar. "We'll see."

13

I arrived an hour early for work and spent it wandering the cemetery across the street reading some of the gravestones. My favorite gravestone was the famous "February 30th Stone," with the inscription *In memory of Elizabeth H. Cullen, born February 30th, 1760*, and the tomb of Captain James Drew of the DeBraak, the English ship which wrecked just offshore. Coins from that ship washed up occasionally after a storm. I wondered how many of those buried here had known the living, breathing Henry.

The church door was open, and the place was empty. No doubt the rector was back in his office, but I was happy to have it all to myself. The air was slightly stale and smelled of wood. I knew the first church on this site had been built in the early 1700s, then a second one in 1808. That one would have been around when Henry was. This was the third one on this site, built in the 1850s.

Sitting in the very last pew, I pondered all the weddings I'd attended here, most recently Kiera's, a server from Half Full, another popular restaurant in downtown Lewes. I was not a religious person and never saw myself being married in a church. I did however, consider myself a spiritual person, which was why I'd opted for the beach. *That* was my sanctuary.

"Miss Vie, can you see me?"

I was so lost in thought I hadn't noticed I was no longer alone. To my left was a very different version of Henry—much more transparent. Not in a whitish, wispy kind of way, like they portray ghosts in the movies, more like he was made of water. Like a really fine ice sculpture. This was disconcerting, and my palms began to sweat as my heart raced.

Nodding, I croaked. "Um, yes. Kinda. Are you ok? Is anything wrong?" I wiped my hands on my pants then tucked them into my coat pockets.

Shaking his head, he continued. "This form requires much less ..." He seemed to search for the word. "Concentration? No, that's not right. Well, regardless, I can stay longer when I'm in this form. Although you look a bit... frightened?"

"No. Nope. I'm good. All good." I think the word he was searching for was *energy*. This form required less energy. Made sense. Still processing that I could now see through him, I whipped my phone out with my list of questions. "Ok, here we go. Tell me your full name and how each one is spelled."

Henry grinned. "You really are too kind, Miss Vie. I am in your debt." Then he spelled each of his four names.

"When and where were you born?" I tapped his answers into my phone.

"November twentieth, seventeen seventy-three, Portsmouth, England."

"Henry…" I feared my next question would cause him pain. "Do you remember anything about how or when you died?" I held my breath. It felt like hours, waiting for his response.

He hung his head. I so wished I could hug him, or say something, anything of comfort. It was all I could do not to slide over and do just that, but hug what?

"I'm afraid not. I remember Sarah was pregnant with our third child." He smiled, yet with such angst, it broke my heart. "That would have been eighteen thirteen, I think."

My eyes stung. "What was she like?" I tapped my phone against my teeth, wondering if he'd mind this line of inquiry.

"Feisty." Henry laughed. He seemed about to say more when he looked over my shoulder.

"May I help you?"

The voice startled me, and I yelped as I whipped around to find a man in a clerical collar standing at the end of the row. He was fiftyish, with an impressive head of pure white hair.

"Gosh, you scared me. I'm um, working on a history assignment." I waved my phone. "I keep all my notes on here, and uh, I dictate stuff to myself—" I fumbled for words.

"Normally we ask that you not make calls inside, but seeing as you're alone and just making notes, no worries. I'll be in my office if you need anything."

As he walked away, I slid down in the pew, wanting to melt into the floor.

"Whew, that was close." I fully expected Henry to be gone when I turned back around, but he wasn't. Still there, in his watery form. "You're still here." It was the longest I'd spent in his presence.

"Yes." Henry frowned at the retreating back of the rector. "A man of the cloth. Not always what they seem."

He sounded annoyed or disgusted, I wasn't sure and I couldn't really read his face in this form. I knew there was more to that story, but also that we were running out of time. Either Henry would disappear or yours truly would need to get to work. I pressed again for his wife's full name, and her details, as well as his other two children, Henry and Edward. I tried to make a joke about the men in his family being restricted to the names of kings, but it fell flat. Something about the rector's appearance had troubled him.

"Oh, crap, I gotta go." I stood abruptly, noticing the time on my phone. "I'll be late for work, I'm so sorry."

When I got up, Henry stood as well. "Of course. Thank you, for your time."

As I reached the end of the row, I turned back to my ghostly friend, hoping to leave on a happier note. "Henry, what was Lewes like compared to Portsmouth?"

He smiled and said, "Paradise."

St. Peter's Episcopal Church

14

"*H*is wife's was named Sarah, and she was feisty," I said, like a proud parent relaying facts about her children. Paris had barely sat when I bombarded him with details of my latest encounter. "And Paris, oh my god, she was pregnant when he died. So, we don't know if she had a boy or a girl or even if the baby survived. Or—"I covered my mouth in horror. "What if Sarah died in childbirth? Oh, shit. Wouldn't that be awful?"

Paris slid his martini back across the bar towards me. "Breathe, child. I think you need this more than I do." The drink tickets behind me spewed out of the machine as the servers got busier.

"But I haven't told you the weirdest part. This time Henry was transparent. I could see through him. It was a little unnerving." I did an exaggerated shudder to make my point. "Not like the ghosts you see on TV. Not the wispy, white things."

"Transparent?" Paris snatched his drink back and almost drained the glass. "Mr. Jell-O was see-through? Oh, no thank you. I don't think so."

I giggled. "Hold that thought." I turned to take care of some new arrivals. When I got back to Paris he was tapping away on his phone.

"Why haven't you called the chef?" He set his cell on the bar and crossed his arms. It was then I noticed the tiny pattern in his green suit jacket were actually little dancing men.

Looking at his phone, I asked, "Why? Who are you texting?" I grabbed for it, and Paris snatched it away.

"Mr. Delicious and I have been in touch. I was very impressed with his culinary wizardry at Space Wars and the client fell madly in love with both him and his food."

"So how do you know I haven't called. Or maybe I'm dating someone else." As if. I dashed off again to retrieve food for a bar regular, then got caught up in making drinks for the dining room. The window seats were considered prime, then the bar, then the tables last of all. All the seats were taken and there was a line at the hostess stand. Maroon 5 played in the background which told me Wick had hijacked the sound system.

As I started to slide a second drink to Paris, I stopped partway to hold it hostage. "Tell me everything if you want to continue consuming libations on these here premises."

"Oh, my funny bunny. You don't think Sticky Wicket," he nodded towards Wick, "won't slip me a drinkie poo when you're not looking? Chef Delicious asked if I'd seen you—says he has a recipe to share. Is that code for something naughty I don't know about?" Paris drummed his black manicured nails on the bar.

"Ew, no. We were just—oh never mind. Do you want something to eat? The mushroom soup is amazing—he started with a Parmesan stock which took it to the next level, and then—"

Paris held up a hand. "Did you drink three espressos before coming to work? What is with you?"

I realized that I was extremely hyper, and not in a fun, caffeinated or jazzed-about-the-world kinda way, but like I was running from something. Then it hit me. I leaned over the bar to talk softly to my bestie. "All the people that Henry ever loved or held dear are dead. And if I find out how and when each one of them died, he'll want to know. As much as I want to help, I dread having that end of the conversation."

15

Paris went home for dinner with his husband, but we decided to meet later at the Library, a new afterhours bar in the lower level of the Hotel Marvil. Those in the know entered through a bookcase that was actually a door. Once inside, the library theme continued. It was a long, narrow space with a scattering of upholstered chairs and an odd assortment of tiny tables that sat in front of floor-to-ceiling bookcases. Soft lighting throughout came from art deco sconces, and a series of world globes lit from within, suspended from the ceiling. Prohibition style cocktails were served along late night nibbles like Philly cheesesteak eggrolls, mushroom bruschetta, white bean pate, and an amazing prosciutto and fig flatbread.

Many of the servers and bartenders from the downtown restaurants congregated here to wind down after work and commiserate over and celebrate our shared experience. Drinks flowed freely, and as the cares of the day floated away, so did our inhibitions. Outsiders might have considered us an incestuous little group.

Jili was the bartender at the Library, and she was good. She was quick, paid attention to who had arrived and when (serving them in order) and wasn't distracted by the number of good-looking men and women who wanted to be her best friend. With chin length black hair with blue highlights, Jili wore dark makeup, almost Egyptian in nature, and had a dragon tattooed on the back of her neck. She smiled easily but wasn't prone to chatting.

I had tried a number of cocktails popular in the 1920s—the gin rickey, the sidecar and my favorite, the Bee's Knees, a simple drink with gin, honey and fresh lemon juice. Now and then, if there wasn't a crowd at the bar, Jili would ask if I'd like to try something different she was working on. It was fun sharing ideas and opinions and learning new drinks as well.

Paris' arrival was always a statement. Either his height, his clothes, or his demeanor often caused a halt in the conversation. He loved it. Arriving just after eleven o'clock, there he stood in a bright yellow suit with matching fedora, mirrored aviator sunglasses, and a walking stick.

I waved him over to the corner where I was happily ensconced in my velvety wingback chair, drink in hand.

As he came across the room, I could easily picture him on the catwalk. I loved my friend. He was flamboyant and fun and unabashedly himself. Also, one of the kindest, most generous people I knew.

Scanning him up and down, I applauded. "Tres chic. And the fit is magnifique."

"Thank you, darling. It's my Nick in Georgetown. I take him a photo from any magazine, and he does it right. Best tailor in Delaware."

"And I just invented a drink for your next soiree. It's called the Electric Banana." I grinned.

"Can't help yourself, can you, Ghost Girl? Lemme grab my cocktail and I'll be right back. Need anything?"

I shook my head and Paris headed to the bar. He and Jili acted like they were old friends, though I knew they'd only recently met. If Paris liked you, he *liked* you.

Paris returned and settled in. Removing his shades, he pointed his cane towards the bar. "Pansexual."

"Who, Jili?"

Paris nodded, sipping his drink.

"What does that even mean?" I had assumed she was straight, but guessing sexual preferences was never my forte.

He held up one finger. "One—it could mean, I'm not sure. Two—don't put me in a box. Three—None 'ya."

I laughed. "None 'ya?"

"None 'ya damn business." Paris smiled. "In her case I think it means she's an equal opportunity employer."

As midnight approached the bar got more and more crowded. Brody from Kindle and Skate from Heirloom cruised by and said hi. Vintage blues played in the background. We scooted our chairs a little closer so we could hear each other. I loved the look and feel of this bar, and the food was sublime, I thought as I scraped the plate to get the last of an amazing black lentil hummus.

"I'm glad you like it." A velvety voice startled me and I looked up to find Niko (aka Chef Bourbon) standing in front of me with two drinks in hand. Jili had apparently told him what Paris and I were having.

I covered my mouth full of food as I said, "Did you make this?" I pointed to the plate of apps.

He shook his head. "No, but it's my recipe."

"It's incredible," I mumbled, trying to swallow. I could see Paris' shoulders shaking from suppressed laughter. I was going to kill him. Clearly Niko was here at his request.

He was dressed head to toe in black and it worked. I felt a strong physical attraction to this man, but the thought of being in the dating realm again made me mentally picture myself running into a room and locking the door. *Nope. Don't think so.* I wouldn't be hurt again. The two men I loved the most were no longer. My father, my rock, had left unwillingly, but my fiancée had simply abandoned ship.

I jumped up. "Here, take my chair." I was about to say I was leaving, when Paris stepped in.

"Oooh, for us?" he asked, taking the drinks from Niko's hands. "Lemme have those. Grab that ottoman, will you, luv?" Paris nodded toward a leather stool that had just been vacated. As Niko went to get it, Paris said softly, "Don't you dare leave, Princess. I got you. And I promise, Chef doesn't bite."

You don't know that. You can't know that. I took a deep breath and closed my eyes. *I breathe in calmness. I breathe out stress.* Reciting these words from my yoga practice over and over, I tried to make myself relax. Sitting down, I smiled as though I wasn't a hyperventilating scaredy cat ready to bolt.

No sooner had everyone settled in when Jili came over with a drink for Niko. A Manhattan, if I had to guess.

Niko explained that he was friends with the owner who had contracted with him to design the menu.

"That hummus is deelish. Next level." I could always talk about food. "Our chef, Cleveland Locke, do you know him?"

Niko shook his head. "Only by reputation." He smiled.

"He just added a mushroom soup that is a complete showstopper. The base is a Parmesan broth, which I'd never heard of." In my nervousness I was babbling, so I sipped my cocktail hoping to slow myself down.

"Yes. I love that base. You use the rind of the cheese, which is completely edible. It's just the cheese forming a protective layer as it ages."

Whoa. Listening to this particular man talk about food was the equivalent of foreplay. It felt more like 'food is my passion' in a sexy way, rather than the egotistical 'of course I know this'. Instead of being annoyed, I almost drooled. Either that, or the alcohol had just hit me. Niko rested his lovely hands on his knees and leaned forward as we talked.

Paris and I both chimed in about our favorite foods: the guac at Agave, the fresh pasta at the Black Rose, the Sea Salt chocolate cake at Kindle. Both of us spoke fluent menu. Niko would prod us from time to time to be more specific about what made each dish special for us, like he was tweaking recipes in his mind. It was intoxicating.

As we finished our drinks, Paris tapped his watch to see the time, then said he needed to get home to his man.

It was close to one a.m. I said I was going to head home too.

"Can I walk you?" Niko asked.

"Um, sure." Bundling up we went out the secret bookcase door, up the stairs and into the dark, velvety night.

16

Although it was mid-November, the temperature was close to fifty degrees. One of the joys of living near the beach. I had read somewhere the ocean warms and cools more slowly than the atmosphere, so coastal weather tends to be more moderate. The streets were empty and quiet, so quiet I worried Niko could hear my heart pounding with excitement.

"Why didn't you call? I think you owe me a recipe."

There was a lilt in his voice that I liked. He seemed genuinely happy every minute of the small amount of time we'd spent together. He also smelled amazing, like woods and rosemary with a hint of orange.

"Well, I'm not sure what Paris has told you about me, but I'm not really dating much at the moment." I looked up at the sky and noticed the stars were especially bright. *Careful, Stewart.*

"And why is that, might I ask?" Every time he spoke, Niko turned his head to look at me.

"Well, a couple of reasons. First, I'm twenty-eight and I think it's time I figure out what I'm doing for the rest of my life."

"Well, what makes your heart sing?" Niko turned to face me.

"My heart sing?" I stared at his eyes which looked very dark and mysterious in the streetlight.

"Yes. That's how I knew that the kitchen was the place for me. When I'm there, my whole-body hums. It's my happy place." He gestured broadly as he spoke and ended with his hands crossed over his heart.

Could you be any more adorable, I wondered. Listening to him talk about food was so gratifying. It was totally his 'happy place.' Niko staring at me made me want to kiss him, so I just smiled and resumed walking. "I'm just not sure. Food is definitely a turn on, as is history. I've also gotten into sketching, although I'd rather keep that as a hobby."

"History, you say? You've landed in the right town."

"Right?" That stopped me. "Lewes is amazing." I pointed to a house to our left. "Like this! The Ryves Holt house. The oldest house in the state. I love how it's a little crooked where the two pieces connect. At one time it was an inn..." And on I went like the proverbial babbling brook.

Too quickly we arrived at my driveway. As much as I wanted to invite him in, have a glass of wine (or two) ... I couldn't. Wouldn't. "Well, this is me."

Niko gazed in awe at the huge Victorian out front. "Nice house. How old?"

"Late eighteen hundreds. It's where I grew up." I pointed to the much smaller carriage house at the end of the driveway. "But presently that's me. And my books." What could I say that might discourage him? "And my six cats."

"Really?" His face registered surprise, but nothing more.

"Um, not really." A forced laugh. I scrunched my face. "I gotta go. Thanks for talking food. That was fun. I owe you." God, I sounded like an idiot. With that I gave a little wave and scurried off down my driveway before I could say anything else.

As soon as I was inside, I texted Paris, *You will live to regret this.* My phone rang a moment later.

"Deeeeeetails. I. Need. Details."

"Nothing happened, my yellow fellow. You ambushed me. And you told him about Logan too, didn't you? He was way too nice. I knew something was up." Lying in bed I put a pillow over my head thinking how weird I'd acted when we got back to my house.

"Darling," Paris said slowly and calmly, "you are my girl. We're not doing a 'Logan' ever again. Not on my watch. Once I knew Niko was interested, I basically told him that if he hurt you, I would come to his kitchen and Gordon Ramsey his ass."

This made me chuckle. "I would pay to see that."

17

On Saturday I made it to the Lewes History Museum around eleven o'clock where someone from the Sussex County Genealogical Society volunteered. She'd been there an hour already, and six people were waiting to chat with her. She looked to be in her seventies, her white hair in a messy bun atop her head with a pencil stuck through it, and big round, red-rimmed glasses. The laptop she clicked away on was covered in stickers, but I was too far away to read what they said.

"Is it always this busy?" I nodded to the genealogy table.

The man at the front desk chuckled. "Oh, heavens no. Just when Imogene is here. She's the best."

"Imogene?"

"Imogene Higginbotham." He looked at her fondly. "She's really something. There's a clipboard on the corner of her desk. You can put your name and number on it, and she'll text you when she's free if you want to walk around the museum."

"Oh, ok. I'll do that."

I had a small sketchbook with me, and as I walked through the History Museum, I thought about what I wanted to tackle next. There was a picture of the Ryves Holt House, built in 1665, that I'd waxed so eloquently about in front of Niko. I was mentally adding it to the list when my phone buzzed. That was quicker than I thought. But it wasn't Imogene, it was Cleveland, our chef.

Down one in the kitchen and Livia isn't feeling great. Can you come in around noon?

Damn. Henry's answers would have to wait. *Sure. No problem.* I typed.

I stopped quickly at the genealogy table and crossed my name off the list. Next to the clipboard were Imogene's cards, so I tucked one in my backpack and left.

After biking home, I jumped in the shower, threw my hair into two messy buns, a quick swipe of lipstick and I was done. If Miley Cyrus could rock the double buns, so could I.

Studying myself in the mirror I was relieved that I'd yet to show a grey hair, and that my skin was in great shape for a beach bunny. Two years till I turned thirty. Jeez. At this point in my life, I'd pictured myself happily married with two kids, a boy and a girl. We'd live in one of the turn-of-the-century duplexes in downtown Lewes with our big yellow lab, and on Sunday mornings we'd brunch at Nectar, tucked away in Neils Alley.

I was sad, though in hindsight glad, that Logan had left when he did. What if we'd married and I'd been pregnant and *then* he decided it wasn't the life for him? I'd rather be single than wish I was.

Looking around my cozy digs, I decided life could be worse. Still, having someone to snuggle with and a reason to take my time getting out of bed in the morning would be nice. My mind drifted to Niko. Even as I pictured his face, I could hear alarms going off in my head. We hadn't had one date, and already I was worried he'd break my heart. *Good grief, Stewart.* The wall around my heart felt impenetrable.

At work, Bad Company blasted through the back door, letting me know Chef was in charge of the music.

"Hey," I said, hanging my coat and stashing my backpack in one of the lockers. "Sous Vie reporting for duty."

Our culinary genius, Chef Cleveland Locke, had his long dark hair in a man bun. I pointed to my head. "Look. We're twinsies. I'd be happy to help graduate you to the two buns look. I think you could pull it off."

Chef picked up a spray bottle of cleaner from one of his pristine stainless counters. "Touch my hair and I'll shoot you."

I raised my hands. "No problem." I laughed. "I smell rosemary. Whatcha cookin'?"

He pulled out a tray of potatoes cut in a way I'd not seen before, like a spiral tornado. They were basted with butter, then covered in a variety of herbs including rosemary, the prominent voice of the dish.

"Ok, not only are they the coolest looking potatoes I've ever seen, they're gorgeous. How did you do that?"

He offered to explain once we'd gotten some of the prep work done, since our line cook had called in with congestion and a sore throat.

Livia, on the other hand, was home with a heating pad and muscle relaxers, having overdone it rearranging the walk-in. She said her back reminded her she wasn't as young as she thought she was, and Chef bitched to me about her messing with his domain.

Slicing and dicing my way through onions, carrots, and peppers, I hummed, then smiled remembering Niko asking me what made my heart sing. We barely spoke as I helped Cleveland prep, happily tasting a new broccoli and Stilton soup, and a side dish of curried cauliflower. He moved in and around the kitchen so easily, so confidently, it was like watching a choreographed dance. Seeing someone so in their zone, was always inspiring. But I also loved people and couldn't see myself tucked away in the back when the front of house was where I shone. Bartending and serving were exhausting at times, and there were always people that you could not please, no matter what. If their day sucked before they walked through the door, there was typically no way I was gonna change that.

My mind wandered to the Library and how magical that whole atmosphere made me feel. The books, the lighting, the coziness of it. Add in the handcrafted drinks and the delightful food—it all combined to create a memorable experience that I loved.

Then there was Niko. I bit my lower lip wondering if he would have kissed me had I lingered in the driveway. Or what might have happened if I'd invited him up.

"Here, let me show you how I did the potatoes." Chef said, as Guns N' Roses belted out "Sweet Child O' Mine" in the background.

Saturdays were our busiest, and as we were all scrambling to cover for the short staff, it never occurred to me to watch the cemetery for Henry till after dark.

18

When I woke up Sunday morning, I had no desire to run or do yoga at the house, or anything that required more energy than refilling my coffee cup and browsing on my laptop. The sun shone through my skylight and I was happily tucked under a huge quilt snuggled in what most would consider an excess of pillows.

Henry had said he came from Portsmouth, so I Googled the town looking for some history. It didn't take long to understand why he felt Lewes was paradise. By the end of the 17th century, Portsmouth was bursting at the seams with more than 30,000 people. From the mid-18th century, those who could afford to do so built houses in nearby Kingston, just outside the noise and dirt of Portsmouth. The dockyard was the main employer and men worked from 6 am to 6 pm. Congested, dirty, and smelly, with a large portion of the town being a marsh, I could only imagine that the Valley of the Swans had been a lovely change indeed.

George III and his Queen visited Portsmouth in 1778, when Henry would have been five. I wondered if he remembered that. Then I thought about being on a ship at nineteen, crossing the Atlantic Ocean with nothing but wind in your sails and the stars to guide you. As romantic as it sounded, I imagined it would have been terrifying, especially in bad weather. I read that the voyage typically took four to six weeks in the late 1700s, people were often ill (definitely seasick), and that below deck smelled awful, which I didn't want to think about. Entering not just a new town, but a whole other continent. Who had he left behind and why did he come? How did he pay for it? Had he known anyone here? Was there a job waiting for him? When and how did he meet Sarah? My mind spinning, I typed a whole new list of questions into my phone.

It felt like weeks since I'd sketched anything, and I missed it. I tried several times to draw, based on my memory, Henry on the bench at Lewes beach, but I threw my attempts away. For me, people were hard. Getting the proportions correct or features distinguishable was such a challenge for me, it took some of the fun out of it.

With the temp in the thirties, I decided I could park my car across from the Ryves Holt House and put my drawing board on the steering wheel. I bundled up, filled a thermos with coffee, and put some fig bars in my pocket for sustenance.

Fortunately, there was a perfect spot available, giving me just the right angle on the house. It was built as an inn in 1665, making it 357 years old. Yowza. Even older than Henry. Ryves Holt, the namesake, had purchased the home in 1721.

Currently the house color was a washed-out blue. Until a year ago, it had always been red which I thought made it more memorable. Therefore, I evoked the artist's right to return the home in my portrait to its original color.

When I looked at the house straight on, it looked like two pieces were connected, and not very well. The part on the right appeared to be sagging, which for me added to its charm.

Between turning my car on and off and my lovely container of java, I kept warm enough to truly enjoy what I was doing. Again, I was grateful my work wasn't being graded or wasn't a necessary part of my income.

Taking a break, I closed my eyes and leaned back in my seat. Despite the heartaches with Logan and my dad, life was good. With Paris and Livia, I felt I had family here. I knew my art would stay a hobby. So what else did I really want to do?

Other options on the table? History? Loved it. But enough to really dive down that rabbit hole, go back to school and get a degree in order to teach? Or work my way into being a paid member of the Lewes Historical Society? I tried this on for a moment. Again, a captivating hobby. I'd even convinced Livia to put Lewes historical facts on one side of our cardboard coasters with our logo on the other. *Lewes was the site of the first European settlement in Delaware, a whaling and trading post that Dutch settlers founded in 1631, and named Zwaanendael (Valley of the Swans).* People loved it—a souvenir of not only their visit to our lovely pub, but a reminder of our memorable town.

I'd learned tons about our namesake, the famous Grace O'Malley, and happily regaled patrons with stories about her. That she was born and raised in a castle and was part of a seafaring family. I also liked telling them that during her reign she personally acquired four more castles either through conquest or marriage. That she spoke Latin as well as Irish and met with Queen Elizabeth. And that she and her crew had quite the fleet which demanded tribute from passing ships, earning her the name "pirate queen."

My coffee was done, and I was getting cold, so I blasted the heater as I drove, feeling drawn to the beach as I pondered a life immersed in history. I pictured myself facing a room full of kids, then teens, then maybe adults, should I choose to teach at the college level. While the thought didn't intimidate me, I didn't feel juiced by it.

It was a full sun kind of day, which almost made me want to put the top down regardless of temp. I missed the warmth on my face. As I parked, I noticed there was no one on the beach, and no one on the benches. Where was Henry when he wasn't here? In the cemetery? Sitting on a bench near the Zwaanendael Museum? When he disappeared, where did he go?

Questions, questions, questions. Maybe, I should become a paranormal investigator. I certainly had the inside advantage. Ha! I snorted.

My phone buzzed. A text from Paris. *Where are you?*

At the beach, pondering my life.

My phone rang. "Yesss?" I drawled.

"Pondering your life," Paris inquired, "what does that mean?"

"Well, I was sketching the Ryves Holt House, then I started thinking about what I wanted to be when I grow up, if indeed I decide to grow up. What about you? Did you always want to be an event planner? Would you want to do anything else?" It surprised me that I'd never asked Paris this question. A bunch of seagulls landed in the sand in front of my car. As if on cue, they turned and faced the wind.

"You know, in my teens I thought I wanted a career in fashion. Not modeling, although I was certainly tall enough, just not pretty enough. I wanted to design clothing and be the next Marc Jacobs. But so much about that industry is cutthroat, and until you're successful enough, you'd always be working for some house like Vuitton or Dior. I wanted to call the shots."

"Well, I think you're pretty enough." I loved Paris' distinctive features.

"Thank you, baby." Paris sighed. "I'm happy for now. Especially when I get clients like Ginny D. Her birthday falls between Thanksgiving and New Year's, and she's hired me to throw a gratitude party."

"A what?"

"She wants people to bring someone to her birthday party that they're grateful for, share why, and have drinks and dancing. She is so damn cute. I love her."

"That's so cool. I'd have to bring you."

Ryves Holt House

19

The fig bars weren't cutting it, so I decided to head to the Station on Kings for some real food. Leisa B was the genius behind this culinary and home décor destination, with its elegant barn building, and an attached greenhouse for dining. They served yummy and interesting food like their crab and corn chowder with leeks and sherry, or their beet salad with cara cara oranges and lemon goat cheese. The Station also sold an assortment of items for the home, gourmet goodies, kitchenware, a wild variety of cookbooks like *Bong Appétit*, and the most exquisite pastries this side of the pond.

It was close to noon on a Sunday, and the place was packed. I got one of the last two-tops in the greenhouse. A few brave souls sat outside, although the propane heaters and restaurant-supplied blankets kept it tolerable. The smell of roasted coffee beans being whirred through a grinder, and bacon frying in the kitchen made my mouth water.

The Stations' quiche was, without a doubt, the best in town. Gruyere cheese, shiitake mushrooms, and caramelized onions, all tucked into an amazingly flaky crust that made my mouth water thinking about it. I ordered that and a latte, and kept the menu with me.

Their chicken salad would have been my second choice, with its red grapes and pecans. This deliciousness was served on a croissant that was a religious experience in and of itself. I studied the menu, as I did at every restaurant, looking for unusual combinations of ingredients, tasting each dish in my mind, wondering if I'd add or delete anything.

Anyone listening to the conversation inside my head would have said, "It's clear you love food. Interesting, really good food. Why not get yourself in the kitchen, or eventually open a restaurant, or something along those lines? Maybe go to culinary school."

Good question, I thought, sipping my latte, just as a woman in scrubs sat next to me. And right then I knew. The realization hit me like an invisible force pressing down on my shoulders. As long as I bartended, which was sort of a place holder, everything was fine. Neither I, nor the universe, considered that my final answer. But once I chose, once I truly became something else … my whole universe would shift. And to what? Because the last thing my father knew was that I was following in his footsteps.

The last thing he knew.

The last thing.

The. Last. Thing.

Whoa. My throat tightened. He had died believing there would be another Stewart, M.D. Another doctor in the family.

I didn't want to disappoint. Couldn't bear it.

20

I drove home, took a long, steamy shower, and curled up on my loveseat with a cup of hot chocolate. Medicine no longer held any attraction for me. Had it ever? Had I chosen that path to please him? Don't know. Why was life so complicated?

He'd been dead six years. Memories of growing up came easily to mind. Our family loved board games, and I remember we were all fairly competitive, particularly my mother, who wasn't above cheating. It was easy to get our parents to play well past our bedtime. Unlike many of my friends, I'd had the luxury of being seen as well as heard. When I was having issues at school, either with homework or a classmate, Dad really listened to what I said, never dismissing it with platitudes like, 'tomorrow's another day', or 'it will all get better', or 'you'll be fine, you'll see'. He was completely present, which in hindsight was such a gift. How could I even think of disappointing this man?

Dad, Finn, and I had also loved being in or around water. Dad had sailing, Finn had surfing, and I alternated between paddleboarding and kayaking. Neither Finn nor I had taken much interest in sailing, but we'd been on Dad's boat enough times to know our way around. It's where I remember my father being the happiest. More relaxed, he laughed easily and often. There was a brightness to him that shone like nowhere else.

Arriving almost an hour early for work, I walked over to the church checking for any sign of Henry. There were a few people near the altar, but no signs of my otherworldly friend. Now that I knew he had more than one form, I considered it entirely possible that although I couldn't see him, he might be there. I called out in a loud whisper just to be sure. Nothing.

I heard the sounds of James Taylor as I came through the kitchen, so I knew Livia was back in action. Our sous chef had returned and was busy prepping sauces for the evening's menu.

My fearless leader sat at the bar, and I went and sat beside her. "How's the back?"

"Much better." Livia made a note on her ever-present clipboard, then turned to me. She was wearing a light blue T-shirt with a stack of books on it with the saying 'No Shelf Control.' I could totally relate. "What's up with you?"

Covering my face with my hands, I looked at her through my fingers. "Adulting is hard. I don't want to play."

She laughed. The music changed to the Rolling Stones and Livia yelled out, "Don't make me come back there," knowing Chef had commandeered her tunes. "Trust me. I feel your pain. Something you'd like to share?"

Easing myself off the stool, I started straightening chairs around the room. "Do you think Dad would be disappointed in me?"

"Genevieve Alexander Stewart." Livia's voice carried a ring of authority.

I immediately stopped what I was doing and almost stood at attention.

Livia patted the stool beside her. "Come back here."

Obeying, I once again sat down. The light coming through the stained-glass windows was glorious, and the smells of Colcannon soup—potatoes, cabbage and onions—that wafted from the kitchen made my tummy growl.

"You couldn't disappoint him in this life or the next. He thought the sun rose and set on you. Why would you say that?"

"Well...I was still pursuing medicine when he died. And now I'm not. And I don't know that I ever will." As soon as that came out of my mouth, I regretted it. Not because it wasn't true, but saying it out loud felt like a sin. Like it was wrong to think it, and even worse to express it. I waited for Livia to chastise me on his behalf.

Out of the corner of my eye, I saw movement. Henry walked by the window, crossed the street, and went into the cemetery. Oh, shit. Shit, shit, shit. Thoughts ran around in my mind like a roadrunner cartoon.

He was in his solid form which meant I didn't have long. But it was such a relief to have the chance to talk about my future with Livia. Maybe she could point me in the right direction. This woman felt like family and had known my father longer than I had. I really, really needed someone to talk to and Livia was making the time.

Sorry, Henry, I thought, turning away from the window.

Then it all came pouring out. "I love food. Pure and simple, I absolutely love it."

"Oh, trust me, I know." Livia's eyes crinkled. "I see you, Genevieve, I do." She sipped her coffee and studied me over the rim of her cup.

"And I'm not talking about dining out—I scrutinize the menus, everywhere I go, taste the dishes in my mind, decide if I think that particular food combination really works. When Chef makes something new, I usually know what spices or ingredients he chose to get there, and if I don't, I love figuring it out." I hopped off the stool and began pacing between the bar and the tables. "But I like front of house as well. It wouldn't do to just be in the kitchen. I like the meet and greet. I like suggesting a wine to go with a particular dish. I, um—" Pausing, I realized I was getting louder and more animated by the minute. "I'm sorry, I don't mean to dump all this on you." I shrugged, not knowing what else to say. I wasn't Catholic, so I had no idea what confession meant, but I felt like that's what I'd just done. This was me being totally honest. This was me, revealing what I truly loved.

"Do you hear yourself? You're so passionate about this— what have you got to lose?"

What *did* I have to lose?

My father's love.

Even though he was gone.

Even though part of me knew there wasn't anything that would stop him from loving me, there was still that fear. Something would be lost.

Livia eased herself slowly off the stool, stood in front of me, and put her hand on my shoulder. "There are no wrong answers here. You can try something on and change your mind. Several of my friends have had more than one career. You're still young. You'll figure it out. I know you will." She pulled me in for a quick squeeze, then turned and went back to the kitchen.

I heard her. Yet didn't.

My father's love.

21

I 'd been out of sorts since seeing the woman in scrubs at the Station, but even more so with the thunderbolt revelation with Livia. There were so many conversations and arguments continuing in my mind that I was starting to feel like someone with multiple personality disorder.

How can you disappoint him?

You're his legacy.

He died believing his daughter was on her way to filling his shoes.

No. No. No. My heart just wasn't in it. Getting a degree in medicine was hard enough. If you didn't really want it, I'd wager it would be damn near impossible.

My father chose medicine. And he chose it for me. Or did he? I adored my dad. If he'd been a fireman, I'm sure I would have picked that. Garbage collector? I'm in. Was it *my* decision to follow in his footsteps? Come to think of it, I couldn't remember a conversation where he'd pressured me to pursue medicine.

At work I was the energizer bunny, which was what I tended to do when I didn't want to think about something. Since we were closing in on Thanksgiving and Christmas, Livia wanted to open for lunch as well as dinner, so everyone picked up extra shifts. We'd also added some temp staff that I was in charge of. This frenzy of activity allowed me to avoid Paris, although he was equally busy with holiday parties. He'd pick at why I was out of sorts and frankly, I was tired of hearing myself.

When my thoughts turned to Niko, I'd grab one of the newbies and show them some of the easier drinks to make, so they could hop behind the bar in a pinch. I hung out more in the kitchen, learning to make the perfect hollandaise sauce, and to watch Chef make a Parmesan base for a mushroom soup. One day when I came to work, there was a package for me about the size of a shoebox sitting on the bar. The wrapping paper was dogs in chefs hats, and the box was tied with kitchen twine. Inside was a lovely whisk, a wooden tasting spoon, a recipe for black lentil hummus, and a note from Niko saying 'Tag. You're it.'

I loved it. So thoughtful, fun, and adorable. Just like him.

Of course, the entire staff was all up in my business after that. Chef threatened to get jealous. Livia, who'd been there when he dropped off the package, said if I didn't want him, she did. One of the newbies, a girl named Bree, was relentless with her questions: "How did you meet him? Have you been on a date? What's he like?" Bree peppered me at every turn. She also stopped up the bar sink because she thought it had a garbage disposal.

"Listen, Newbie, unless you want trash detail and the job of taking out the floor mats and hosing them down every night, I suggest you cease the Spanish Inquisition and get busy wiping down the menus." Our menus were laminated, and we wiped each one every single day.

"A Spanish what?" Bree's eyes widened.

I suddenly felt old. Bree may have been twenty-one, but she was a young twenty-one, with wild, chin length curly red hair that almost looked electrified.

"I pointed to the menus. Get busy, Red."

At home that night, I carefully folded the puppy paper as a keepsake, then I hugged the box. Paris had given me gifts from his travels. Little rings from different countries or some delicacy in a tin. But his trips were few and far between. So, presents were a rarity in my life, and it felt really good to get one that was an acknowledgment of my interests. 'I see you', it said.

22

"You know, your dad didn't always want to be a doctor." Livia smiled slyly. "He actually fancied the theatre, then films. Wanted to be the next Tom Hanks." She wore a shirt featuring an image of Mt. Rushmore with the words 'we will rock you'.

"Are you serious? He never said anything." Some vague memory of him on stage in a yearbook swam fuzzily in the background. Per my usual, I'd come in early, deciding that I needed to dust every one of the bottles behind the bar.

"He was amazingly good in high school productions. Very funny. No stage fright."

Just then Chef brought out two small bowls of butternut squash soup. I held it to my nose and closed my eyes. "Oooh. I smell sage. Yum." A quick taste. "And is that ... apple?"

Chef fist bumped my shoulder. "That's my girl."

Livia studied my face. "It won't be medicine for you, will it? I and everyone else around you can see where your heart is. Your father's family chose medicine for him. He was good at it and learned to love it. But he would want *you* to choose for *you*."

Her phone rang. "Oh, I need to grab this." She patted my hand and went back to the kitchen.

My dad an actor. Wow. Yet I could kinda see it. He was gregarious and charming with a wicked sense of humor. Growing up, he made the funniest faces and wasn't afraid to fake a fall to get a laugh out of me or Finn. When he read books to us, he'd make up a new voice for each of the characters and put his whole body into the performance. If we hosted a party, guests orbited around him, enjoying his clever repartee.

The holidays made me miss Finn, miss having a family, and miss being in a relationship. Both Livia and Paris had invited me for Thanksgiving dinner, but I declined. Paris would be heading to Maryland to be with his family, and Livia always invited the orphans and strays to her house. Neither was appealing in my current state of frustration.

By eleven on Thanksgiving Day, it was a balmy sixty-four degrees. Deciding I needed to clear my head, I ran to the beach, then plopped on the bench where I'd last seen Henry. Despite the gorgeous weather, there was almost no one here, not even a seagull. I pictured everyone tucked in a holiday decorated home, surrounding a table straight out of a Norman Rockwell painting. A little too Hallmark for me, but my mother loved it.

"Miss Vie, I trust you are well?"

I almost jumped off the bench. "Henry," I said, holding my hand to my heart. "You're here." Well, kind of here. He was in a state somewhere between solid and the ice sculpture-y watery version.

"A favorite place." He nodded towards the bay. "I love being near the water. Lewes is a far prettier sea town than Portsmouth ever was, at least in my memory." He smiled and turned sideways on the bench, resting one arm on the back.

I hung my head. "I'm afraid I don't have any answers for you just yet, I—"

Henry raised a hand to stop me. "Please, don't think of this as your life's mission. These answers have eluded me for so long that it's a pleasure just being able to share that with you. That you are attempting to help me is a genuine gift. But more importantly, being able to converse with you warms my soul."

A flock of geese flying in the standard V formation streamed overhead. I felt both happy and sad to see him. Sad, thinking about him not being with his family, then me not being with mine. Happy to be with him as something about his energy, his presence, always reminded me of my father. I was glad that I was someone who could see him and that we could talk.

"You seem troubled, have I disturbed?"

"Oh, no. Not at all." I shook my head. Then my emotions swelled unexpectedly. "Oh Henry, it's just—" I covered my face with my hands, trying to contain the flood that threatened to sweep over me. "Life is just—" I jumped up and began pacing in the sand. Then I stopped myself and tried to calm down.

Henry had stood when I did, which I found utterly charming. "What can I do?"

Deep breath. "Please, sit. My father was a doctor. He died six years ago, while I was studying medicine. I was planning to follow in his footsteps." I paused, looking out at the lighthouse on the horizon.

"Then you must. There's still time." Henry leaned forward on the bench.

I ran my hand through my hair. "I'm not sure it's what I want. But I'm afraid if I don't, he'd be so disappointed."

"Ah." Henry smiled and sat back. "Henry, my first born, had no intentions of becoming a carpenter as I was. By eighteen, he was already a man of the sea, hoping one day to captain his own ship."

On the bench once again, I sat sideways, hugging my knees. While standing on the beach, I'd noticed a few more people had arrived, so I put my earbuds in with the wires visible and tapped my ears from time to time so that it appeared I was on the phone.

"Does that help you hear better?" Henry inquired, pointing to my earbuds.

"Ha! No, they're connected to my phone." Did he have a clue what that was? "I don't want people thinking that I'm talking to myself since they can't see you."

"Oh."

From the look on his face, I guessed he didn't understand some of what I just said, but I wanted him to continue. "Were you disappointed that Henry didn't join you? I mean, your son, Henry. Did you both go by Henry?"

Henry laughed, shaking his head. "No. We called him by his third name, Edward. He was an excellent carpenter, too. And you are correct. I believe every man wishes their legacy to continue, whether it be through children carrying the family name, or delving into the family business. But when I witnessed the joy on my son's face every time a ship came into harbor, I knew I couldn't be the person who said that's not for you. Even when he was just a lad, boats filled him with such excitement. I realized that perhaps it was my own needs, my own fear of not doing enough in my lifetime to make a difference in the world, which made me want him to continue my legacy. But that's not his burden. Nor his journey. That was my own."

Inside my mind I saw a tiny ray of hope break through a mass of very dark clouds. How could my dad be disappointed if something other than medicine made me truly happy?

Henry was starting to look a little more transparent. Uh oh. I pointed at him. "I think we may be running out of time. Can I ask, how does it feel when you disappear and where do you go?"

He shrugged. "It's as if I suddenly fell asleep, then I wake up standing in the graveyard near your tavern."

"Wait. You always 'wake up' there? That must mean something Henry. Maybe you are buried there."

"I don't think so. You had to be a member of that church and I definitely wasn't." He looked unsettled.

"Then maybe you died there. Or near there. Do you remember where you lived? Was it close to town?"

The sun went behind the clouds. Henry once again appeared to be made of water. I could see the bench through him.

"We could walk from the farm, but it was a ways. Maybe five miles. We usually rode a horse or brought the wagon if we needed supplies." He smiled. "My boys loved any excuse to come to town or be near the water. Both could swim like the fishes. And both loved the ladies. Oh my, did they love the fairer sex." This made him chuckle.

"Did they marry before you—"

Henry was gone.

"I can't see you Henry, but are you still here?" Nothing. I reached over and tentatively patted the bench where he'd sat. Gone.

Though I was once again by myself, I no longer felt alone.

23

My third Thanksgiving dinner invitation had come earlier that morning, but I once again declined. That afternoon, I carefully unpacked the bag of goodies Chef had sent home the night before. There was mushroom soup, my new favorite, and Shepherd's Pie. Then mashed potatoes because even though that's a part of the pie, you can never have enough. His rockin' gravy. Caesar salad with dressing on the side. And pumpkin cheesecake. Yowza.

While I was heating things up, I poured myself a glass of Farmhouse, a red blend that was my current fave, and stood in my window watching people arrive at the big house. My house, truth be told. My childhood home that I'd lived in since I was ten years old. Once Finn left, and my mother moved to Florida, there was no way I was going to stay there by myself. So, I rented it, and moved to the carriage house in the back. The couple living there had two small children, and they'd offered the third invite for Thanksgiving dinner, if I hadn't any plans.

The house was a grand old thing, two stories tall, white siding with black shutters, and a big front porch that wrapped to the left side. The right side had a huge bay window that my mother had made our breakfast nook. The kitchen had been modernized, but still had the original tin ceiling. Gorgeous stained glass above the front door and side panels. It had been built in 1895 and belonged to a sea captain, his wife and their four children.

There were pocket doors between the front parlor and the dining room, and I remember thinking they were the coolest thing ever when my father showed me how they disappeared into the wall. There were three fireplaces, and the bathroom adjacent to my bedroom had floor to ceiling white tiles and a clawfoot tub. Being cast iron, it kept the heat, and I could stay in there 'til my skin wrinkled, and my mother shooed me out.

Since Finn had had a treehouse, my parents allowed me to set up my own space in our ginormous attic. I used an antique folding screen to help define my territory, and covered the wood flooring with every rug I could find. Despite the ceiling height, there was only one window, so it was a bit dark. Using a trunk as a table, I put three mismatched lamps on it so that I'd have light to draw or read by while sitting in a low-slung beach chair. With a few of my favorite stuffed animals as company, I was happy.

Looking out the window, I sipped my wine as I thought about my childhood.

Did their kids love the attic? I hoped so. I knew the screen was still up there. A lot of the furnishings were ours, but we'd removed all of our personal items. Except the artwork. My mother was constantly buying art at every craft show and festival, so we had enough to start our own gallery. Sailboats painted all different ways as a nod to my father's passion. A line drawing of four older women at the beach. A rainy night street scene in a large city. All different mediums, all different styles. I picked my favorites, had them carefully wrapped and stored, and left the rest for the tenants.

Around seven my phone buzzed.

"Hey girl," Paris said in his deep, radio voice. "Gobble, gobble. Whatcha doin'?"

"Hold on, my mouth is full," I mumbled. "Enjoying my favorite of Chef's creations."

"Oh! Is Niko there with you?" Excitement filled Paris' voice.

"What? No. I meant my favorite dishes made by Cleveland, silly. Not—oh, never mind."

"Damn. I was getting all sweaty over here."

I could visualize Paris fanning himself.

"I'm so glad I don't live close enough to see these people that often. They're my family and I love them, but girrrrrrrl, they cannot stop talking about their health problems, their money issues, relationship disasters. I feel like I'm on a reality show and it ain't pretty."

I laughed as I watched the young family come out to greet an elderly couple.

"You seem distracted. Should I let you finish that shepherd's pie? Or is it the mushroom soup you can't stop talking about?" Voices in the background rose, as did whatever was on TV.

"Good grief. It sounds like you're at a bar." It was bittersweet watching the family assemble for the holiday.

"Welcome to my world, honey. But what's going on? You've been ghosting me again. Did we break up?" Paris mumbled 'no thanks' to someone in the background.

"Ha! No. Just the usual. I'm still thinking about going back to med school." I held my breath, feeling queasy just saying it.

"What? You. Are. Not. If I could reach through this phone I would slap you into next week. When did this start? You haven't mentioned that in years." Paris tsked.

Did I really want to get into this? My resolve was tenuous at best. "I dunno, Paris. I was at the Station. This woman came in dressed in scrubs and all I could think of was that I didn't want to disappoint my father."

"Girl, stop right there. Reverse the situation. Pretend you're a surgeon in her fifties with two children, one in med school. If that child decided for whatever reason that being a doctor wasn't her jam, would you be upset?" I heard ice clink in his glass.

"Well, no. Not upset. But probably disappointed. I—"

Paris interrupted. "Would you want your child to pursue medicine to make you happy?" He said each word as if it was its own sentence.

"Can I call you when I'm done eating?" I asked, though I'd lost my appetite.

"You better."

I didn't.

24

Exhausted by the talk about my future, I tried to get my mind to focus on sketching. I'd taken a class at the Rehoboth Art League that introduced me to a group called Urban Sketchers. They had chapters all over the world, including my home state. The Delaware group had around 400 members with all ages and skill levels. They met once a month, rotating their meetings between the three counties. The international Urban Sketchers Facebook group however, numbered 116,000 people. I could scroll through their posts for hours enjoying the use of color, the fine detail of some of the penwork, or others' use of quick, broad strokes. On their personal pages they often discussed their preferred tools of the trade. Blackwing pencils came up often.

Our downtown Lewes bookstore, Biblion, was awesome. Owner Jen had packed so much fun in a small space, I hardly knew where to start. I'd seen Blackwing pencils the last time I was there and decided to treat myself.

As it was just a few blocks from my house (catty-corner from Grace O'Malley's), I walked. Biblion sat on a corner with windows on two sides. It was housed in a turn-of-the-century building, with an old-fashioned glass door that made a satisfying clack when you opened it. The shop was a combination of new and used books, the world's best greeting cards, an eclectic assortment of journals and notecards, and a very sweet dog named Nellie. Oh, and Blackwing pencils.

Fellow artists I followed call them 'affordable luxury'. There were four different sets, each with a different purpose, so I opted for the fifteen-dollar set that contained one of each. Neither Jen, the owner, or Nellie, the tiny black mop with four feet, were present, so I didn't linger. Also, the Black Friday shoppers were beginning to arrive and I wanted to be in and out early on to beat the crowd.

The downtown shopping area in Historic Lewes was small but fun. There were several restaurants including Half Full, which made the best prosciutto and pineapple pizza, Notting Hill Coffee (or Amy's we locals call it) which had excellent coffee and their 'ooey gooey' pastry which sold out quickly, the Lewes Mercantile (an antique gallery), an assortment of boutiques, a toy store, bank and more.

I wandered up and down Second Street, happily noshing away on a cranberry-orange scone from Amy's, then sauntered over to First and sat by the canal while I sipped my coffee. I'd never seen Henry here, but looked for him anyway. During warmer months, fishing boats, tourist boats, and the occasional kayak zipped up and down the waterway which connected the Broadkill River and the Delaware Bay. It was built by the Army Corps of Engineers in the early 1900s.

It occurred to me that when Henry arrived, the canal wouldn't have been here. At that point it was the much smaller

Lewes River. Wow. I couldn't imagine the changes he'd seen over two hundred and fifty years. Were those changes slow enough to be intriguing, or fast enough to be frightening? Personally, I would have loved it. At least, I thought I would. If I could have had one superpower, it would be the ability to time travel. Not to live in any time but the present, but have the ability to stand, let's say in front of St. Peter's cemetery, and wind back, fifty, one hundred, or two hundred years, to see the changes. Horses to cars. Hoop dresses to yoga pants. Mannerisms and conversations. Changes in storefronts. Henry had seen it all.

I thought about sketching the church and the cemetery, but it was too close to work, and I didn't want to be anywhere near Grace's. With all the extra shifts, I was there more than I was home.

There were a few of the turn-of-the-century lifesaving stations around the area, small shed-like structures that once held rescue equipment used by volunteers in case of a shipwreck. I could sketch one of those. The closest one was located next to the Lightship Overfalls. Huge double doors on one side opened onto a ramp, so the volunteers could send a small boat out to assist a floundering ship. I said small, but the life-saving surfboats accommodated eight rowers and weighed over 2000 lbs. The Lewes station also contained a life-car which looked like a mini submarine. My father had loved all of this and had been fascinated by sea rescue stories.

My father. *I never imagined my life without you*, I whispered. *Every part of Lewes reminds me of you.* Maybe it was time to move.

Wait, what? Where the heck had that come from? But why not? Finn was in Hawaii, my mom was in Florida, who said I had to stay here? Just sell the family house and move on. Forget medicine, forget bartending, just go reinvent yourself somewhere else.

Run away, Stewart. Run away.

25

The Saturday after Thanksgiving I was at the Lewes History Museum at 9:55 a.m. That way, I'd be first in line for Imogene Higginbotham, and hopefully, get Henry some answers.

At 10:02, the doors were finally unlocked by a tiny woman bundled up like Nanook of the North. She blocked my path. "Oh, dear, I do apologize. We don't seem to have any heat in the building. I'm afraid we can't open."

"Oh, okay. But is Imogene here? I just wanted to ask her a quick question." I danced from one foot to the other trying to keep warm and be patient.

"I'm so sorry. The genealogists are only here every other Saturday. Have a good day." And with that, the gatekeeper closed the door.

Wait, what? "Crap." I swung my backpack off my shoulder and dug through the front pocket trying to find Imogene's card. Not there. Stomping to my car like a petulant child, I wrenched the door open, got in and dumped my entire backpack on the passenger seat. Rifling through my stuff, shoving some of it onto the floor, I cursed aloud. "Shit. Fuck. Dammit." Frustrated, I pounded on the steering wheel. Life sucked.

*   *   *

Between Thanksgiving and Christmas, I worked liked a crazy woman. At the pub, I was on autopilot, trying to convince Livia that I was most likely going to return to college and continue into medicine, and I was fine with that. I don't think I was fooling anybody. At home my apartment was the cleanest it had ever been, and I'd reorganized my bookshelves more than once, donating a few things to the library. I even started cleaning the garage, a task I'd neglected for far too long.

I hadn't seen Henry, but I hadn't really looked for him. Ok, maybe now and then I'd give a glance at the cemetery, but I had nothing to report. Truthfully, I'd not made the effort. Maybe a part of me worried if I solved the puzzle of Henry's family—if I tied up that loose end for him, his time would come to a close. And no part of me wanted that to happen. I didn't know him well and yet the thought of losing him... I couldn't.

This was always an interesting time of year. A rush of out-of-state visitors coming in to shop tax free Delaware. My locals who loved Christmas and were happily prepping for it, came to the bar less. Those who struggled with the season, came in more. There was less middle ground—people were either exceptionally cheerful or silent. I got it. Christmas for me had gone from a raucous family gathering—that my father delighted in, watching Christmas movies, hanging strand after strand of outside lights, and my mother never decorated any less than five trees—to nothing.

My mother. After my dad passed, she confessed that seeing me reminded her of him. That we had the same nose and smile, but I also had his laugh. And it broke her heart to hear it.

Every year she invited me for Christmas. And/or New Year's. And every year I declined, claiming I needed to work. True, Livia needed all the help she could get, though I knew if I pressed, they would have covered for me.

*   *   *

Christmas Eve the pub was packed, but with more of those who struggled with the holiday for one reason or another. Some of the normally chatty regulars were suddenly quiet. Some drank more than usual. Some shared photos of family they had hoped to spend time with, but for whatever reason, could not. There were a few weary shoppers, and a smattering of familiars who dipped in for a quick drink and a moment of escape from family.

I chatted with everyone I knew, making sure I squeezed an arm as I handed them a drink or something to eat. Listened intently to stories. Hugged them long and hard when they got up to leave. This was my extended family. A community I knew well and loved.

The staff was exhausted, but we'd announced earlier in the month that we'd stay open till midnight. I had on bell earrings that jingled as I worked, along with a headband with reindeer antlers. Chef had found a rockin' Christmas music station, and was outdoing himself in the kitchen, comforting our patrons with consistently great food like his potato leek soup, cheesy mashed potatoes and homemade cranberry sauce with mandarin oranges.

My holiday drink creations were wildly popular, particularly the Apple Blitzen, an alcoholic version of a hot apple cider, and the Naughty Nog, an eggnog martini with not only bourbon, but rum and whisky as well.

By ten, there was no longer a steady stream of people, and I paused to catch my breath. Stepping out the back door, I looked up at the night sky, and smiled as a few snowflakes fell on my face. It wouldn't be a white Christmas, but I did love snow. Chef had stepped out for a cigarette break.

"Did you always know you wanted to cook?" I asked, still looking skyward.

Cleveland snorted. "Didn't have a choice. My dad left when we were young. My mom worked two jobs, so my Nana hauled my ass into the kitchen." He shook his head. "You would have loved my grandmother. She was a pistol." He took a long drag. "Took no prisoners. Even though she was shorter than Livia, nobody messed with her."

I tucked back inside and was surprised that several empty seats at the bar were now full. No sooner had I caught up on one side, I turned around and there sat Paris and Niko. Wick had just set their drinks in front of them, and I noted that Niko was sipping a Naughty Nog. Turning my back to them under the pretense of helping someone else, I texted Paris.

You gangbanger! WTH?

His great booming laugh echoed down the bar.

Knowing I couldn't avoid them forever, I sauntered over. "Hello, boys." I rested my hands on the bar in front of them. It occurred to me that this was the third time I'd seen Niko and every single one of them I was in bartender attire. The man had no idea how great I looked in a dress.

"This is the one." Niko pointed to his nog. "This is the recipe I want."

I swore his eyelashes were even longer and thicker than the last time I'd seen him, and he smelled like spices used in Indian cooking.

"Oh, reallllly?" Smiling mischievously, I turned to Paris, who was dressed head to toe in a shimmering suit and cape, the palest of blues. "What's up, Elsa? No parties this evening?"

Paris ignored my comment on his attire. "We just finished a holiday/birthday party. The birthday girl turned eighty-five years, and at nine o'clock, she told everyone to leave, as she was going to bed."

Both men chuckled. Niko sipped his martini and made the look that I do when I'm trying to determine the ingredients.

Paris continued. "Now mind you, this was after three hours of drinking, dancing and karaoke. Birthday girl was rockin' the Janis Joplin tunes. Niko's spread was amazing. It was a round the world tour, with an emphasis on Indian food."

"What did you serve?" I turned to Niko. His hands rested on the bar. Nice hands. Beautiful golden skin.

Ignoring my question, he pointed to his drink. "Nutmeg for sure, but something else. Cinnamon. Maybe vanilla?"

I shrugged. "Maybe. But Wick made that one. I'll make the next." And off I flounced. Scooting back to the kitchen, I noticed my heart was beating faster than normal. "Damn that Paris," I said under my breath.

"Gosh he's cute." Bree cruised behind me with a tray of dishes.

He was indeed. I didn't need any complications in my life, and I didn't think this would be anything casual. I didn't want casual with this man. And that in itself frightened the crap outta me. I wanted to sit and talk food for hours. I wanted my hands in those dark black curls and that gorgeous mouth on mine, and...

"Need your help." Wick nodded to me and our line cook.

I knew that look. Someone had had too much drink and we had to get them out. Unfortunately, this wasn't New York City, and we couldn't just sling them into a cab. But we did have Uber—it just took time. And it wasn't enough to escort them out the door. They'd walk right back in.

Heading towards the dining room, Wick paused. Paris and Niko had their arms around a fifty something man, who seemed very absorbed in their conversation. Both loomed over him by several inches, and they were slowly escorting him to the door. Then outside.

Within minutes, they were back.

"Thanks, guys." Wick reached over and shook their hands. "Appreciate the help."

Niko smiled, looking directly at me. "No problem. A few of my friends drive for Uber and one was close. Happy to assist."

Behind the bar my knees softened. What a delicious man. Inside and out. I slid my version of Naughty Nog across the bar. For my favorite patrons, I made mine with bourbon, rum and cognac, instead of whisky. "On the house."

Niko slowly sipped, then closed his eyes.

I could see Paris' shoulders shaking and I knew he was suppressing a laugh. I pointed at him and mouthed, *Stop*. He slid his empty glass towards me. "I need some naughty too."

Niko tapped his glass. "You *will* give me this recipe. You *owe* me."

"Yeah, I suppose I do." Resistance was futile. I wanted to give him much more than a recipe. Oy. Mariah Carey sang "Santa Baby" in the background. Bree must have hijacked the music.

"I'm going to make it into a dessert. A crème brulee, I think." Niko smiled, and it had a bit of mischief behind it.

"Oh god, that would be amazing," I blurted like a fangirl without even thinking. "I mean, that's sounds incredible." Clearing my throat, I turned to some newcomers, but Wick was closer, so I refocused on my two amazing gents.

"Did you guys want food? Kitchen's still open."

Both men shook their heads. The volume in the bar had gradually dimmed without me realizing it. The stools at the windows were empty, and Bree, bless her heart, had already cleaned those bar tops. I glanced at the cemetery and wondered if Henry was there in the dark. Alone.

"We're heading to the Library for one more, and you're coming with us." Paris pointed at me.

"Oh, I can't—"

Wick stepped behind me and put his hands on my shoulders. "Look, Vie. You've done your fair share this month. Bree and I got this. Go." And he pointed me towards the kitchen.

Within minutes, the three of us were at the Library, along with half the wait staff and bartenders that worked in downtown Lewes. Some of us had families to go home to, but for many of us, this *was* family.

Niko bought the first round, and despite my protests, Paris bought the second. Then my tall, shiny snowflake said he needed to get home to his husband.

"I'll make sure she gets home safe," Niko said, placing a hand over mine.

Oh my.

I stood and hugged Paris, kissed his cheek and wished him a Merry Christmas. And just like that, Niko and I were alone. I slid down in the upholstered chair so I could lean my head back on the cushion. "Where's your family?" I asked.

"Mostly in Greece. One older sister in New York." He studied the rocks glass in his hand. Jameson.

I was grateful he didn't ask about mine.

We sat there in silence, which actually was more comfortable than I would have imagined. Then I leaned forward. "I think I'm done for the night."

He smiled. Nodded. Then drained his glass.

We walked in silence most of the way to my house. Colored lights shone through the windows. Elaborate wreathes with iridescent ribbons, glitter-covered pine cones, or miniature toys hung on hundred-year-old doors. Owners of Second Street homes, many of which had been owned by pilots, outdid themselves. Decorated trees covered with thousands of tiny white lights. Strands of pine looped around railings. The smell of wood burning fireplaces. Pausing at a corner to let a car pass, Niko wrapped his scarf around my neck and tucked my arm through his. There was a light dusting of snow on the ground, but it had stopped, and a full moon lit the sidewalk like a supernatural night light.

Pausing at my driveway, I was suddenly aware of how physically and emotionally exhausted I was. Then I noticed the lit and decorated tree my tenants had placed in the bay window breakfast nook. "Oh," I gasped, putting a hand to my mouth. My mother had always put one there as well. I looked away, knowing I was about to cry.

Niko wrapped himself around me and kissed the top of my head. "C'mon. Let's get you inside."

I nodded, afraid to speak, fearing I would come undone. It had been six years since I'd celebrated Christmas in the big house.

As I pulled the keys from my pocket, Niko gently took them from my hand, held them up to the moonlight and guessed the right one. He followed me up the stairs, and after I turned some lights on, removed my coat and gently laid it on the back of one of my kitchen chairs. Then he led me to the loveseat, sat me down, removed my boots, and covered me with my nana's quilt.

For whatever reason, all I could do was watch.

Niko found a bottle of red, a corkscrew and two glasses. He pulled out his phone and the next thing I knew, Etta James was playing through the tiny speaker.

I raised my glass to him. "Thank you," I mouthed. The moment felt both sad and magical, and I felt if I said anything, it would ruin it. So, I just sat. Closed my eyes. Listened to Etta.

When I finished my wine, I padded off to the bathroom, brushed my teeth, slipped outta my jeans, came back out and got in bed in my T-shirt and underwear. Niko followed suit, turned me on my side and tucked in behind me, curling himself around my body like we'd done it for forty years.

Then, we slept.

26

Christmas morning, I woke to the smell of coffee and something else amazing.

"Merry Christmas," said my Greek god, raising his coffee mug in my direction.

Sitting up, I gave a little wave, then noted the cup on the nightstand beside me. Cream. Hopefully no sugar. Taking a sip, I was pleased he'd guessed right. Grabbing a pair of jeans on the way to the bathroom, I went to make myself a little more presentable.

Minutes later, I emerged to find my little table set, and an omelet calling my name.

Niko had a dish towel on his shoulder, which he used to wipe his hands, then joined me at the table. Leaning back in his chair, he sipped his coffee slowly, then sat his cup down. Black. How did I know?

"Please tell me you eat breakfast." He laughed, then dug in.

I nodded as I took a bite of the gorgeous egg dish before me. Then I moaned. "Ohmigod. What did you do to these mushrooms?" I asked, with my mouth somewhat full.

"I cooked them in wine and butter and added a little salt. Pepper. Tarragon."

"Tarragon," I whispered reverently. He'd also found my gruyere and grated it on top. I couldn't remember ever spending this much time with someone, especially someone I didn't really know, and saying so little. It was almost spiritual. And really, really cool. It was so comfortable I almost laughed out loud. But instead, I just smiled. At one point, I refilled our coffees, took the coffee press back to the counter and was returning to my seat, when Niko reached out and grabbed my hand.

I stopped, turned, and sat in his lap. Then I caressed that lovely face in both hands and kissed him.

A minute later, he carried me back to bed, where we happily spent the next two hours.

Best dessert ever.

27

I had no idea Niko had turned his phone off, but when he turned it back on, it buzzed like angry bees. Glancing at all the texts, he said, "I'm so sorry. I have to go shop and prep for a dinner this evening. Merry Christmas." He kissed my nose, then my cheek, then long and softly, my mouth.

Still, I had no words. The last twelve hours had been totally unplanned and unexpected. I didn't want to ask, *so what does this mean?* because I had no idea. If I opened my mouth, I feared the wrong thing would come out. So, I just smiled and watched him get dressed.

"I'll call you later."

I nodded.

Niko gave me a little wave and was gone.

I pulled the covers over my head and screamed and pounded my legs on the bed like a teenager who'd just met Harry Styles.

What the hell had just happened? And that was it. It just happened. Miss, 'I gotta control everything' had just gone with it. And how delightful *that* had been.

I texted Paris. *Is the Doctor in?*

He called me fifteen seconds later. "Spill, girl. I need deets."

I took a very deep breath, then let out a long happy sigh. "Doctor? I think there's been a breakthrough." Then I started giggling.

"Are you drunk, little one?" Paris sipped on something. Coffee maybe? An early Naughty Nog? I could hear gospel playing in the background.

"In a manner of speaking. Niko spent the night." I opted not to share that we'd first slept together without having sex, then had sex after breakfast. There was something so special, almost sacred, about the fact that somehow Niko knew I needed to be held more than anything, that I wasn't ready to divulge specifics.

Paris screamed. There seemed to be a lot of that this morning. Then I heard him tell Rafael that he was fine, and that I got laid.

"You know, it wasn't just getting laid. It. Was. Fabulous. No, incredible. Something. I have no words." I threw the covers off my head.

We chatted another ten minutes or so, then I promised to stop by later for drinks and dessert. I really wanted to see him. I wanted to embrace my orchestrated family. I wanted to be out in the world.

28

I took a long, leisurely bath, using every expensive soap, cream, and whatever that I own. I shaved my legs. Something I wish I'd done sooner, but ah well. I spent time on my feet as though I cherish what they do for me every day. Then I decided to drive to Rehoboth, and walk the one-mile Boardwalk while I sipped my hazelnut coffee.

On Route 1, a car with Jersey tags decided they were not in the right lane, and swerved in front of me. Slamming the brakes, I narrowly avoided hitting it, but that meant everything on the passenger seat ended up on the floor. Normally an obscenity would have rolled right off my tongue, but today I just shook my head and continued on.

Once I parked, I went around and collected everything off the floor mat. And there was a small white card peeking out from underneath. It was for the genealogist. Imogene! I was back on track. Were it not Christmas, I would have texted her.

Henry. In my Niko afterglow, I thought, *I haven't forgotten you, but you've certainly been relegated to the back.* I wondered how he would have celebrated Christmas with his family. Did they decorate? Would there have been gifts? Especially with a new baby in the house. It was unbelievably sad that he hadn't gotten to experience that. Despite my fear that he might disappear if I discovered what had happened, I made it my number one New Year's resolution to find his answers. What a wonderful gift that would be.

I had layered up for the cold, as it's always cooler by the water. The sun was bright, and there were more people than I had expected strolling the boards. Many of them only got to experience this one or two weeks a year, but the ocean was here for me every day. I was happy about that. Feeling ridiculously alive, I walked the entire length twice before I parked myself on one of the white benches. Some face the ocean, others the boardwalk. But I knew that the back of each bench could be flipped to face whichever way I pleased.

When my father died, he was cremated. We held a ceremony and scattered his ashes at sea. We'd known it was his wish after a conversation at the dinner table one night.

My mother had volunteered with several organizations, one being Lewes in Bloom. This was a group who, years earlier, had planted thousands of bulbs and plants throughout the historic downtown area. Now there were flowers everywhere. The group had over 200 volunteers who had continued to expand and maintain the planters, baskets and gardens, receiving the America in Bloom awards at least three times.

While serving supper, Mom had relayed a story about a downtown planter being moved that had caused an uproar. A local Lewes woman had buried her husband's ashes in it, and had no idea where he'd gone. We found this both sad and hilarious, and it led to a discussion as to how we'd want our bodies handled.

My mother's family had a plot in a cemetery near Wilmington, Delaware, and she expected to be buried there. I remember being curious that she wouldn't want to be near my father, until he said he wanted to be cremated and buried at sea. Finn echoed that sentiment, while I wanted to donate my body to science. My mother hated that idea but didn't elaborate why.

My father went on to say that to be buried at sea, you had to be taken at least three miles out, and if you used an urn, it had to be biodegradable. He also said that ashes scattered at sea are like sand. They do not float. They do not dissolve and will descend into the ocean until they hit the floor.

The fact that he was so knowledgeable about this left us all dumbstruck for a moment until my mother switched the conversation to something else entirely. Had he known then he'd die way too young? Like Henry?

Regardless, it was impossible not to spend any time looking out over the vastness of the Atlantic and not think of him. The wind had picked up and created larger waves that crashed upon the shore. Closer in I scanned for dolphins, then further out I noticed a container ship on the horizon. I loved he was a part of something he loved so well.

My phone buzzed. It was Finn.

"Wassup, my bro?" A seagull screeched over my head.

"Are you sitting by the ocean, oh sister of mine?"

"I am indeed. And thinking about Dad."

I tipped my head back. The sun felt amazing on my face. Always did.

29

Paris opened the door attired in a white silk shirt, black pants and a red sequined smoking jacket.

"I feel underdressed," I said, putting my hand to my chest.

"Get in here, princess." He laughed as he pulled me through the door.

There was a Disneyland feel in his foyer, as there was almost too much to see and take in. The walls and ceiling were painted cobalt blue. On my left was a mirrored console table with an elaborate holiday bouquet; on my right a giant mirror with wavy sides. Further down the hall there were more mirrors in all shapes and sizes and mirrored mosaic animal heads jutting from the wall, wearing sunglasses. Appropriate as light bounced around the hallway everywhere.

I turned to face the squiggly mirror now framed by a hundred or so white lights. "Mirror, mirror on the wall ..."

"Girrrrl, you know that bitch is not going answer anything other than 'Paris' or I will take it out in the backyard and ax it to shards." He took my hand and led me down the disco corridor. The long entryway opened into a two-story room where floor to ceiling windows overlooked the backyard. We'd moved from Disney to Vegas. The center piece of this great room was a bedazzled silver piano on a slightly elevated stage. Rafael plays beautifully, and I was hoping he'd oblige me later.

Above the piano was a giant chandelier that waterfalled from the ceiling. It was at least ten feet from top to bottom, with dozens of cascading crystal globes of light. The walls were painted a charcoal gray, but the art was such a riot of color that the room felt anything but dark.

The two exceptionally long couches were tufted in dark purple velvet, and the accent chairs were lime green. Sounds a bit garish, but with the right pillows (of which there are dozens), it really wasn't. Paris called his style violent elegance.

The dining room table was a glass top, supported by two gold statues resembling the man on the cover of Atlas Shrugged. It sat twelve. Half of said table was now covered in pastries and desserts. I recognized many of my favorites made by Phoenix, a mutual friend who was a renowned pastry chef. Pumpkin scones drizzled with lemon frosting, a walnut and honey baklava, coffee filled cream puffs, Vienna apple strudel...

I whipped around to Paris. "Who else is coming?"

"Well," he said, slipping a fan from his sleeve and snapping it open to fan himself. "I thought you might bring a friend. Henry? Oh Henry, darling?" Paris looked around the room.

"Oh, very funny." I turned and began piling my plate. Then I helped myself at his built-in coffee maker/espresso machine. Not only had I been here before, I'd bartended here and knew where everything was.

I plopped on one of the velvet sofas and leaned back. Rafael arrived from another part of the house.

"Hello, my precious," he said, kissing me on both cheeks. "Sorry. Work called. I have to go to Thailand to look at a property next week."

He was dressed in all black. T-shirt. Jeans. Slippers. He was slightly shorter than Paris and had thick, black hair that was shaved close on the sides. Mustache and beard in that two-day growth look. Lean, but muscular. Quick to laugh. One of my favorite things about him.

Paris returned with a bloody Mary.

"I could have made that," I said.

"You're our guest, sugar," he purred. "And how is Henry? Or better yet," he leaned forward. "How is our Niko?"

I think I blushed from head to toe. Clearing my throat, I squeaked out. "Fine."

Both men cracked up.

Paris sat his drink on the table and picked at a croissant. "I like him for you. He's gorgeous, kind, intelligent, and knows what he wants. Unlike the noob that left you on the beach."

"And he speaks food. *Fluently*. My favorite language." I put my hand over my heart, ignoring Paris' remark about my ex.

Paris pressed for more details, but I remained vague about my time with Niko. I wasn't sure what it was, or what I wanted it to be, but most importantly, I didn't want to overthink it like I always did.

"And how's our ghost?"

Rafael sat up straight. "Ghost? What ghost?"

Paris patted his knee. "Oh, my love, I know how you feel about these things, so I haven't really shared, but our Vie is friends with a spirit."

I was surprised, but pleased Paris hadn't shared my spectral friend with the planet. I didn't want to have to explain to everyone in our circle, and I also didn't want everyone thinking Vie was certifiable.

Rafael stood and began pacing. "My grandma's house was haunted by something. We all felt it and to this day, I don't like talking about it." And off he went.

My mouth fell open.

Paris shook his head. "You know how you have a major dentist phobia? Well, everything woo-woo is off limits with my honey bun. I shouldn't have said anything in front of him, but I feel like we haven't caught up in forever and you won't give me any dirt on Mr. Delicious." He sat back, crossed his legs, and straightened an already perfect crease in his pants.

"I haven't seen Henry in a while, but I did find a genealogist whom I'm hoping can help." I sipped my cappuccino, enjoying the sound of the cup settling on the saucer. Blues played softly in the background on well-hidden speakers.

"Are we referring to Imogene Higginbotham?"

"How did you know?" I felt bad that we had scared Rafael out of the conversation.

"She's the go-to-genie in these here parts." Paris stirred his bloody with a long swizzle stick topped by a large jewel.

I laughed. "The go-to-genie? That's hilarious."

"You'll be waiting awhile. She's in hot demand, and not just Sussex county. More like the entire state."

That wasn't good news. I'd call and text her first thing tomorrow and find out where I was in the queue. "How are you doing? Business good?" I revisited the buffet to restock. Suddenly I was ravenous.

Paris was quiet and when I returned from foraging through the table of deliciousness he was staring out the window.

"What's up, Buttercup?" I said softly.

"Tomorrow is Prague's birthday. He would have been thirty-eight." Paris closed his eyes.

Paris was the youngest of five boys, all named after international cities. His mother had cleaned offices most of her life—her favorite being a travel agency. She'd bring home the glossy brochures she'd found in the trash, studying them for hours, naming each of her babies after the places that called out to her.

We'd been robbed. Both of us. A beloved parent and a treasured older brother, taken by rage. It left you violated in a way you can't explain to someone who hasn't had that experience. I placed my hand on his knee and left it there.

30

I texted Imogene Higginbotham at nine a.m. the day after Christmas, then wondered what I was going to do for the rest of the day. It was Monday, and Livia had decided to close the restaurant Mondays and Tuesdays till March. We just didn't have enough staff to open seven days a week.

Based on what Paris had said about Imogene, I was hopeful she'd be able to help me with Henry's family. Every ancestry database search I tried came up empty, and on my own I was getting nowhere. Thinking about this, I wondered where Henry might go if the holidays were hard for him. Maybe the church? No, more likely the beach. I vowed to search for him that afternoon.

Perusing my TBR (to be read) pile of books, I thought about going back to bed with my cup of coffee. Or maybe adding Kahlua to that coffee. Or texting Niko to see what he was up to. Niko. I stretched like a cat, then hugged myself. My body felt good just thinking about that man.

As if I conjured him, my phone buzzed a moment later. *Have time to play today?*

Did I ever.

We agreed to meet at the Lewes Oyster House at three, so back to bed I went.

I left early enough to go to the beach, driving by each bench slowly, looking for Henry. Except for one lone car, the parking lot, the sand, and all the benches were empty.

I was sitting at the bar at 2:55 when Niko strolled in. He was such a presence. Tall with his dark, wild mane of curls, Ray-Ban sunglasses, black cashmere overcoat, black jeans and boots. He looked like a celebrity, and more than one head turned to watch him walk across the room. Squeezing my arm, he settled beside me. Today he smelled like pumpkin pie: Cloves; nutmeg.

"You look delicious." He took my hand, then turning it over, kissed my palm. "May I order for us?"

At that point I would have said yes to anything. "Please," I replied, sliding the menu his way. I was wearing a sapphire blue and black striped sweater dress that came to mid-thigh. It had a scoop neckline and showed off my curves. I also had on black tights and short black boots, wore my hair loose and had used a new floral scented shampoo that smelled amazing.

Niko slid the menu away without even a glance. "We'll have the Lobster Corn Dog and some peppers," he said to the woman behind the bar. She smiled and nodded as she put his drink in front of him.

"Jameson on the rocks?" I guessed. "And what peppers?"

"Shishito. They're charred. You'll like them, I think."

Though it was clear our bartender had an interest, Niko did not. It did my heart good to feel like no one else in the room mattered but me. Really good. As each dish arrived, including my cocktail, he made me close my eyes and inhale slowly. Then he wanted to know exactly what I could smell. I named everything I could. *Anything else?* he'd ask. Then, eyes still closed, he fed me a tiny bite of each one, and asked me again to describe the initial taste, then the one that lingered after I swallowed. Then he'd kiss my lips very slowly and softly before he'd allowed me to open my eyes once again.

It was arousing and fun at the same time. I smelled and tasted things differently with my eyes closed. That was interesting. Then we'd discuss each dish, ingredient by ingredient. Would I change anything?

We repeated this at two more restaurants in town, each time ordering two appetizers and a drink. Then the tasting. Oh, the tastings.

In between I learned that everyone in his family cooked, from grandmother to mother to father. He even had a sister who was a baker. And they were all opinionated as to methods and seasonings. He said dinner at his house would sound like a riot to an unsuspecting guest.

More than anything, he wanted to open his own restaurant. It would be a fusion of sorts. I had to laugh to myself. Some of us in the industry upon hearing the word fusion from a new restauranteur took this to mean that the chef had no idea what to cook. But with Niko, who had experience in New York kitchens and now his own catering business, it meant the freedom to serve more of what he pleased.

I could talk food all day, every day. Not only was I tremendously attracted to this man physically, I wanted to crawl inside his head and luxuriate in his food knowledge. It was as sexy to me as his dark eyes and gorgeous curls.

We ended up back at my place, peeling off each other's clothes before I closed the door, and making love on the living room floor. Then we curled up together in a blanket on the love seat, sipping red wine and listening to the blues.

I had no idea of the time, nor did I care, as I had nowhere to be and wonderfully, neither did he. He asked if he could spend the night. Absolutely, I thought, but just nodded. I loved that he didn't assume. That we didn't fill every minute with questions and conversations. We had talked nonstop and intensely all afternoon and into the evening as we tasted our way around the town, but now we just had to be. It was divine.

He woke before me once again, and coffee and breakfast awaited as I made my way over to the table. He'd somehow managed French toast with a blueberry drizzle from the random items in my fridge. A girl could get used to this.

As I sat there looking at him, I didn't want to think about what this was. I was desperately trying to stay in the moment as I hadn't felt this cherished or relaxed, in well, forever. This was nothing like my relationship with Logan. For one, Logan hated silence and would talk about nothing to fill the void. The only thing he was passionate about was baseball, something in which I had little interest.

"What are you thinking?" Niko leaned forward, cup in hand, elbows on the table.

"Trying not to, actually." I smiled, leaned back in my chair and tapped my finger against my mug. "Enjoying how comfortable I am. And happy."

Niko noticed Imogene's card on the table. "Are you tracing your family tree?"

"Mmmmm... not exactly." It was the first time I'd been coy with him. "Helping a friend," I explained, but it didn't feel authentic, and the air changed.

"I'm sorry. I don't mean to pry." He frowned like he'd overstepped.

God. How could I explain Henry? Or did I even try to explain Henry? I covered my face with my hands. Should I change the subject? Talk about my career choices instead? Arrrrrrgh. *Stop.* I thought. *Just stop.* Everything that started to come out of my mouth felt wrong. I didn't want to spoil the mood or the moment, but all of a sudden, all my insecurities and the life decisions I'd been grappling with, came marching into the room, demanding attention.

"Are you ok? Should I go?" Niko reached for my hand.

No. Don't go, I thought. *Unless you want to.* I stroked the top of his hand but didn't say anything.

He wove his fingers through mine. Crazy thoughts ran through my head, almost tripping over each other to come out of my mouth. How much I liked this man. And it scared me. How I feared disappointing my dad. My incredible, larger-than-life father, whose ashes we scattered to the waves. And then there was a ghost I could see that no one else could. I laughed out of nervousness.

He tugged on my hand, pulling me out of the chair and onto his lap. Then, he wrapped himself around me and held me. "There's a lot on your mind, I get it. And you can tell me anything, or not. Or we could just talk about food for the next fifty years, it's all good."

I nestled in and let out a huge sigh. It could all wait. For right now, this was all I needed.

31

When I woke, the bed was empty, as Niko hadn't spent the night. Not sure why, maybe he'd felt I needed my space. I still wasn't sure how much to share with this man. No, I take that back. I wanted to share everything with this man, and I found that frightening. With so much loss in my life, I didn't want to set myself up for more disappointment. I'd been weird after he picked up Imogene's card and retreated into myself, which was the first discordant vibe in our relationship. Or whatever this was.

My phone rang then. It was Imogene. I had added her number to my contacts, in case I lost the damn card again.

"Hi, this is Vie."

"Genevieve. Yes, I know who you are, and your father too. He was my sister's surgeon for which we are forever grateful. I'm so sorry for your loss."

I was temporarily speechless while I processed this information. "Yes, um. Thanks."

"How can I help?"

I loved the confidence in her voice. "Well, I was trying to find out more about a Lewes man and his family. His name was Robert Talbot and he died around eighteen fifteen. I tried Find-A-Grave and Ancestry but struck out." *And by the way he's a ghost.* I bit my lip waiting for her response.

"Is he a relative? I'd love to help but I'm terribly swamped. Apparently, I was the Christmas gift du jour. People purchased an hour of my time as a present to family and friends. It's a wonderful compliment, but it's becoming a full-time job."

"Oh, I understand. If you—"

"Well of course I want to help the daughter of our favorite doctor." She cut me off. "It just might be a few weeks before I can get started. I'm sorry. Did you say the gentleman was related?"

"Uh, yes. Yes, I think so." No, I decidedly did not. But if it got me to the head of the queue, I'd use my father and anything else I could.

"I'll text you my email and you can send along any information you have that might help. Toodles." And she was off.

Related? I stared at my phone a moment, then set it down carefully like it was about to bite me. *You lied, Stewart.* I'd sent her off in the wrong direction. Well, I could always clear that up in the email. It was a relief we'd finally connected.

Slightly annoyed with myself, I pulled out a few of my drawings to see which one I wanted to try and finish. Flipping through them quickly, I ended up shoving the whole pile on the floor.

Had I blown it with Niko? Hopefully not. Maybe. What was wrong with me?

Frustrated, I layered up and decided to go for a walk. It was warmer than I thought, and I was soon loosening the scarf I'd wrapped so tightly around my neck. I knew if anyone could find answers for Henry it would be Imogene, so that was a good thing, right? I could now report progress if I saw him. But I didn't want Henry to go away. I didn't want Niko to go away. It occurred to me that my fear was making me act like someone I didn't know.

32

Downtown Lewes was rather quiet that morning. Very few cars and almost no people. I sat on a bench in front of King's Ice Cream, now closed for the season, and faced the church and the cemetery.

"Good morning, Miss Vie."

A faint watery outline of Henry sat beside me.

"Henry—you surprised me. You're more transparent than usual. Is everything ok?" I put my earbuds in then took them right back out. Screw it. I no longer cared what people thought.

"Oh, my yes. I've found that I can hold this form the longest. Is it too unsettling?"

It was hard to read his face, but I could hear the concern in his voice. "No. Nope. Not at all. It's fine. I finally connected with a genealogist. Miss Imogene Higginbotham. It might be a while, but I'm hoping she can help." I was still irritated with myself that I hadn't been more persistent when I really cared about Henry.

"That is truly kind of you."

A car drove by with the stereo turned up and the bass thumping all the way down the street.

It occurred to me that he might not understand. "Henry, do you know what a genealogist is?"

"I'm afraid not. But I'm ever so appreciative of your efforts."

"They trace the descents of families. Their lineage. Much of that information has now been collected into one place..." how would I explain online? "And Imogene is considered one of the best." Now that I was still, it was colder than I thought. I shivered inside my coat and tightened my scarf.

"That sounds wonderful. In my day lineage was very important among the royals." He paused. "Is there anything I can do for you, in kind?" Henry's voice was calm. Reassuring. Kind of like my dad's. I could hear him in my head asking me, 'What's up, Buttercup? You good?'

"Well, there's this guy I like. And I don't want to blow it, but ..."

"How does one blow it?" Henry inquired.

I laughed. I wanted to tell him about Logan leaving me at the altar which messed with my mind for future relationships, but I didn't want to explain why or have Henry think badly of me. Would he assume I'd been unfaithful? Why else would a man not choose to be with a woman in his day? I decided to reframe my dilemma.

"Henry," I continued, "a gentleman is courting me." I smiled as I said this 'Henry-style,' knowing it would please him. "I like him very much."

"How wonderful! Is the young man gainfully employed? And what is your opinion of his family?"

"Henry, you sound like a dad." I liked it, actually. My father would also pepper me with questions, and left more than one of my high school dates quaking in his boots.

Mrs. Reese walked by with her dachshund, Nugget, stopping right in front of me. "Good morning, Genevieve." Nugget appeared to be looking at Henry. Could dogs see him?

"Good morning. Hi, Nugget." I reached down and rubbed his ears. "Who's a good boy?" Fearful Mrs. Reese would join me on the bench and sit on Henry, I stood as though I was leaving.

"It's chilly today, don't you think?" The older woman looked up at the sky. "C'mon boy. Happy New Year." And off she toddled before I could respond.

"Henry, can dogs see you?" I sat back down with my translucent friend.

"Sometimes, I think."

How cool, I thought, yet dogs are open to their senses in a way most people have forgotten to be. "Has anyone ever sat on you?" I laughed. Couldn't help myself.

Henry chuckled. "Oh, heavens, yes. But they almost immediately rise as though they sat in something."

"They can feel you as I did?" This surprised me.

"I don't think so. They often comment about the bench being wet," he paused. "Now. About your young man." He crossed his arms. Again, something my father would do when the conversation turned serious.

"My young man is a chef. I've not yet met his family as most of them live far away. But he's charming and kind. I think you would approve." If the two of them met, I believed Henry really would like him. I'd noticed when Niko was in his business mode, he was much more formal. Like the first time we met at Paris' event. I think that politeness, that respect, would resonate with Henry. Niko also feels very genuine to me, no guile—and I think Henry would admire that as well.

"If he pleases you, Miss Vie, I'm sure I would. Affairs of the heart can be..." Henry appeared to be searching for a word. "As I told you, my Sarah was feisty." He smiled. "Her parents felt they'd already made a suitable match. I wasn't their first choice, you see."

I so wished I could see his face clearly. He was adorable talking about her. I could hear the absolute love and joy in his voice.

"I'd built some beautiful cabinets for their home, just over there, actually." He pointed down Market Street between the cemetery and Grace O'Malley's. "There were servants so we were never completely alone, but we did manage to have conversations almost every day. She was delightfully curious about everything: what wood I was using and why I had chosen it, the name of each tool, how well everything fit together. It made what I was doing feel like the most important thing in the world and I loved her for it. She also read voraciously, much to her father's chagrin. He felt she was neglecting her needlework and piano forte."

"So how did you win her?" I asked.

"Well, as luck would have it, the young man they had in mind received a very desirable job offer in Philadelphia. Sarah was an only child and her mother was distraught at the idea of her daughter and grandchildren living so far away. I made my intentions known to her father, by that time a great admirer of my work, and fortune smiled upon me."

Philly wouldn't feel far away today, but back then, I suppose it did. I couldn't imagine all the changes he'd seen and asked him how he felt about it. "Mixed," he said. Sad that so many of the homes, shops and inns familiar to him were gone, and that everyone he'd known had long passed.

Looking across the street at the cemetery, I wondered how many of his friends and family were buried there. He was the last man standing.

On the flip side, Henry marveled and was delighted by inventions, particularly engines. Motorized vehicles and boats fascinated him. As we spoke, a helicopter that flew overhead both tickled and terrified him. He couldn't understand how something that large kept from plummeting to the ground. I didn't try to explain. I'd taken these things for granted for so long, I knew I'd have to Google how planes actually did stay in the air.

I could have talked to Henry for hours. Days even. Everything we mentioned took us down a new road of conversation. The library, for instance. A building full of thousands of books? That *anyone* could borrow at any time? It thrilled him immensely. His joy in all the things I took for granted gave me fresh eyes and an even greater appreciation for my lovely Lewes.

33

To the staff's delight, Livia had started dating the Walrus, and began to travel. This was surprising to me as she'd always been married to the pub. I was happy but jealous at the same time, dancing around my own relationship with Niko. Livia also brought in an excellent bartender that she wooed away from a Rehoboth restaurant, in order to give me the reins to manage the pub.

Manager. I'd been unofficially placed in that capacity several times over the years, but this was the real deal. Official title, raise and all. She'd shadow me till we both felt comfortable and confident I was ready to be on my own, as Livia wanted more time to play. But more importantly, it afforded me the chance to experience something I might want to do for the rest of my life.

I learned the ins and outs of working with the various food suppliers, the liquor reps, placating kitchen staff, scheduling, and payroll. With Niko and Paris less available, I jumped in with both feet. Livia was terribly pleased, and said I was a natural. It was crazy and exciting how much she was willing to hand over, but then, she was having the time of her life with her George. A win-win.

I'd gotten a text from Imogene saying that she was finding Henry a bit of a challenge and that she needed his wife's last name. I checked my notes but couldn't find that information anywhere. If he'd given it to me, I'd lost it, and I was never sure when we would find each other again. Every day that I was in the pub, I'd spend my break in the cemetery looking for him.

Paris had joined his honey bunny in Germany, then France. He and Rafael decided to extend their stay for two more weeks, wining and dining their way around Europe. My bestie was buying so many new clothes, he had to ship them home.

Thanks to Paris and all his connections, Niko's popularity was growing by leaps and bounds. Paris had touted Niko's culinary skills to anyone and everyone he knew, and for good reason. Niko had a gift. He began to put a business plan together to court potential investors for his restaurant, which meant his free time was severely limited. Mondays seemed to be the best day for us to connect, so he'd often come over late Sunday after I closed O'Malley's.

We'd open a bottle of wine, have a drink or two, then head to bed. Or if we were particularly wound up about the week, talk into the wee hours of the morning.

One particularly chilly morning we were having a hard time leaving the down comforter and the warmth of being naked and wrapped around each other. "What are you going to name your restaurant?" I asked, snuggling into his chest. I loved the feel of him, the smell of him. Woodsy. Herbal.

"I thought about naming it after my grandma, Sofia, who I spent the most time with in the kitchen, but I think some people would assume it was an Italian kitchen. My favorite though, is just Olive."

I propped myself up on an elbow. "I love that. It's simple but elegant, somehow."

Niko sat up as well. "Right? Definitely says Mediterranean." His phone buzzed but he ignored it. "I love planning the menu, playing with dishes and variations. But my apartment is a mess right now. Looks like the home of a mad scientist." The sun shone through my skylight, highlighting the amber strands in his dark hair.

"Is that why I haven't seen it?" I asked, scooting out of bed to head to the bathroom. Oops. Was that too pushy? What if he had a sexy roommate? Or a Fifty Shades closet?

"Well, your place is always so neat, I didn't want to freak you out. I can be tidy, um, sometimes." He slipped into his jeans and went to the kitchen to make us coffee.

Oh dear. Was he a hoarder? "I clean when I'm stressed," I confessed. "I love running Grace O'Malley's but it's a lot of responsibility and I don't want to disappoint Livia." Slipping into a T-shirt and yoga pants, I opened the fridge door, though I knew it wouldn't be pretty as it had been weeks since I'd done any serious shopping.

"Are you related?" Niko paused with two mugs in his hand.

"To Livia? No. But she's the closest thing I have in Lewes to a relative."

He'd put the cups down and was now behind me, resting that gorgeous head on my shoulder as he too gazed into the vast wasteland known as my empty fridge. "Hmmm… I love a challenge, but…" he laughed, then his hands found their way under my shirt, then down my pants. When I gasped, he flipped me around and kissed me passionately. Next thing I knew we were on the floor, and when I sat up twenty minutes later, I laughed because the fridge door was still open. No complaints.

Niko suggested we go out for breakfast, but I had laundry to do and needed to restock my pantry. All the things I'd neglected while I managed Grace O'Malley's.

While I loved testing my wings as manager, I had slowly allowed it to consume me, and used it as a place to hide. But the minute I closed the pub for the night, I was miserable inside. On my days off, I'd find myself there, reviewing schedules, wondering how I could run things better, or cleaning and organizing parts of the restaurant that I felt had been neglected. This meant I wasn't reading or sketching, two things that fed me on an entirely different level. Physically, Niko and I were having great fun, but emotionally I was holding him at arm's length. We'd talk food and restaurants, but nothing deeper. Nothing about my past with Logan, or relationships, or how we felt about marriage or children. My sense was that he wanted more, and I thought it only a matter of time before he moved on.

It occurred to me that I was ghosting the people that I loved. Appearing and disappearing in their lives at random according to my fears. And I missed Henry. He provided a sense of calm—a tether when the world swirled around me.

Something had to give.

34

The Lewes Historical Society had moved into the old Lewes library space once the new library was built. Between the two buildings, they placed a caboose on a small piece of track as a nod to the railroad history of the region. I'd heard they'd also acquired an engine but wasn't sure when it was coming.

Though I'd been at the pub till midnight, I woke up earlier than usual on Sunday morning and decided to walk the mile to the library and draw the caboose. I knew something in my life needed to change. I needed less Grace and more balance. Along the way I grabbed a coffee and a cranberry orange scone, happily noshing my way along Second Street, eager to return to my art.

Some early walkers were already on the trail adjacent to the library. It looked to be a gorgeous day. Not a cloud in the sky. The air was crisp but with no wind it felt warm enough to enjoy the outdoors. I walked around the caboose, taking shots from every angle with my phone. That way I could work on the sketch later. I also might see another angle I liked better and change the direction of my piece.

People were walking and talking on the trail as bikers whizzed by. I smelled someone's fireplace from one of the Victorian homes across the street from the library. Settling on the closest bench, I pulled out my pen and sketch book, and drew an outline of the big shiny red piece of history parked in front of me. I loved trains and hearing about the changes they'd brought to all the little beach towns. One of my favorite stories was how boardwalks came to be. In the 1870s, everyone visiting walked on the beach. A railroad conductor and a hotel owner got the idea to construct a boardwalk as a way of keeping the sand out of the railroad cars and the hotels. At that time, they just put down a walkway of boards then picked them back up in the winter. Now boardwalks are permanent. Lewes didn't have one, but Rehoboth's was a mile long.

Taking a deep breath, I closed my eyes and tried to empty my mind of all the angst I'd been struggling with for the past few weeks. The sadness of missing Henry. My fears around letting Niko in. Managing the pub. I just wanted to sketch and not think about anything else. Lose myself putting pen to paper. Maybe think of an interesting story or some drama that may have unfolded around this caboose. I tried doing that sometimes with what I drew, finding it fun to let my imagination run wild with stories that may or may not have been true.

"Miss Vie."

I was startled by the sound of Henry's voice. "Oh, Henry! I'm so happy to see you." Well, sort of. Henry was in iceman mode. I wanted to say 'how are you' but that seemed like an odd conversation to have with a ghost. I mean, he was dead. How would I think he was? "I need your wife's last name. I thought I wrote it down, but I couldn't find it, and I've been in touch with the genealogist, and…" All this came out in a rush.

"It's lovely to see you as well. How are you, really?"

"I'm fine," I said, a little too quickly. Trying to be fine. Wanting to be fine. I didn't want this man feeling he had to listen to my troubles every time he saw me. I pictured him with his boys, and imagined he was a fun, attentive and thoughtful father. Like my own. "You're very kind and I appreciate your concern. There's just some things I need to figure out on my own." I stared at the little red caboose. "Henry, have you ever even been on a train?"

"Yesss."

He said this like a boy admitting to stealing sweets from the candy store.

I whirled to face him. "Did you sneak on board? No ticket? You sound guilty. What's that about?" Of course he snuck on board. No one could see him. By the time trains came to Lewes, he was already dead.

Henry burst out laughing. "I did," he said. "I was close enough a couple times when it stopped, that I just stepped on." He chuckled softly. "It was glorious. Then of course, the train passed my boundaries and whoosh, I woke up in the cemetery once again."

"So, when you say, you woke up, what exactly does that mean?"

"It's like I fell asleep, but I don't remember falling asleep. Then I wake up, always in St. Peters graveyard." Henry watched as a young family strolled by—a mom, a dad, and a toddler who paused to gawk at the big red caboose.

"What form are you in when you wake up?" I used my fingers to indicate quotes around the words wake up, then realized the toddler, a girl with curly red hair, had turned to stare at me. I waggled my hands like moose antlers along the side of my head, made a face and stuck my tongue out at her. She frowned, put her thumb in her mouth, and wrapped her chubby hand around her mother's pant leg. Mom patted her absentmindedly on the head, and the trio moved along down the asphalt trail. I turned to find Henry studying me.

"Will you have children one day?" he asked. "Forgive me, if that's impertinent."

Despite just scaring one, I said, "Oh Henry, I hope so." And I meant it. Logan had been on the fence about it, but I'd wanted a tribe. Then they'd always have each other no matter what life threw at them. Though when my dad was murdered, Finn hadn't handled it well at all and I'd never felt more alone. "Henry, did you have siblings?"

"A much older brother. He worked on the docks." Henry looked down at his shoes.

I noticed for the first time that there didn't seem to be a left and right shoe. They both looked exactly the same. He didn't offer anything further on the subject.

"You mentioned boundaries?"

"Oh, yes." He explained that the church seemed to be his center, and from there, he could go as far east as the Bay, north to New Road, west to the Lewes Library, and south to well, not sure where he was describing.

"And what happens when you try and go beyond those lines?" This had to mean something.

"It's like I'm no longer conscious until I arrive back at the church." He sighed.

"Huh. Interesting."

"Have you ridden a train?" Henry asked.

"Oh, yes. Many times. It's my favorite way to travel. I love being able to walk around while the train is moving. Go from car to car. Watch the countryside fly by." Indeed, I'd traveled with my family up and down the East coast. Even the auto train to Florida which meant that we spent the night on board. My dad had splurged on the Family room with two big picture windows. It had seating for four that transformed into two upper and two lower beds at night. Finn and I had top bunks. We'd loved it.

"Have you ridden a..." Henry hesitated, then pointed skyward.

Smiling, I said, "Yes, I've flown in a plane." My mind wandered to traveling with my parents, and I could feel my heart swell as I shared these memories with Henry. We had spent time in Portugal, Spain, Italy, France, Mexico, and Canada. Travel lit up my mother. Any sense of adventure and she became her best self. Engaging. Funny. Charming everyone she met. And they loved her right back. Being with my mother as we globetrotted held my most favorite thoughts of her, and I was very animated and happy as I described her. Suddenly, I realized that Henry had become more solid beside me. He was totally absorbed in our conversation and had a sense of awe on his countenance. "Henry, what is happening right now? I can see you better."

"Listening to you talk about these experiences—I can't describe it. I feel more—alive, I think." He shook his head. "No that's not right. I'm hardly alive." For the first time I heard an edge to his laugh. It felt forced.

"You get juiced. More current. Um—" How did I put this in his vernacular? I snapped my fingers. "More wind in your sails!"

"Exactly." His face lit up and he nodded, his icy blue eyes wide open. "More wind in my sails. That's stating it perfectly, Miss Vie." He leaned back against the bench and closed his eyes. "I miss the sea. I mean, I know I can still see it, but to be out on that vast body of water, the boat rocking with the rhythm of the waves, the mist, and the wind on your face. There's nothing like it."

It was how my father had described sailing. It fed his soul in a way that nothing else had. A feeling of peace settled over me.

"Did you not think about a career that would keep you at sea?" I tucked my sketch pad back in my satchel. Henry was the reason I was meant to be here. This was a good man. A kind man. He loved being a father and he loved the sea. All of this my heart could relate to.

"A career? Oh, the work I did? Absolutely. But once I found my Sarah and had the boys, I couldn't bear to leave them. There was much demand for carpentry. Sarah's father was well known and well respected, and his reputation helped mine tremendously." He crossed his arms. "That, and I never did work that I wasn't proud to call my own." As he said this, he sat taller on the bench.

"Are there things you built that are still around?" I turned sideways on the bench with one arm over the back. I avoided this sometimes when talking with Henry, because it made it more obvious that I was having a conversation with someone that wasn't there.

His face clouded. "Some of the pieces I made were in St. Peter's church. But those disappeared long before they built the current structure." His visage faded and he resembled the iceman once again.

"Henry, you've faded again. It's fine. I don't mind you in any form. I'm just an intensely curious person and you're the only ghost I know." I put my hand to my mouth. "Is it ok that I'm calling you a ghost? Does that offend you?"

"It does not. Sadly, I think that is what I am."

35

I hadn't done much sketching that morning, but it was ok. I loved the opportunity to spend time with my ghost. For whatever weird reason, the universe had said, "Vie – I think you need a spirit in your life – HA!" And you can see him, hear him, and no one else can. And you can help him find his family. And parts of him remind you of your dad. Which, when I thought about it, stunned me: maybe Henry was the one helping me find my family.

Or maybe I was just truly and certifiably crazy. But I'd *touched* him. Put my hand through his fucking ectoplasm, or whatever the heck he was. Right?

Maybe I'd made up all this supernatural drama to avoid making decisions about my own life. Maybe what I should have been doing, instead of spending time with people who weren't really here, was to get serious about the rest of my life.

I'd always believed that marriage and children would also be a part of that life, but what if they weren't? The men in my life leave. My dad. Logan. Even Henry wasn't permanent. But Paris hadn't left, I reminded myself. My nearest, dearest friend was still here.

I got to work twenty minutes early and found myself wandering in St Peter's cemetery. I ventured inside and immediately heard voices. As my eyes adjusted to the darker surroundings, I noted a man of cloth chatting with two older women. They finished up as I stood there, so I wandered over to the man in black.

"How can I help you?" The white-haired gentleman inquired. He had gold wire rimmed glasses that he kept pushing up his nose.

"Do you know what the clergy would have been called, for this church, I mean," I pointed down, "back in the early eighteen hundreds?"

"Hmmm…" he removed his wayward glasses and rubbed them with a well-worn hankie from his pocket. "I'm pretty sure it was 'reverend' at that point." With his glasses back in place, he peered at me intently. "Are you doing research?"

"Kinda." I wasn't sure why I was asking him this, it was just the first thing that popped into my head. I remembered reading that the second church built on this site had been completed in 1808. Henry was still here. Maybe he'd help build it. Maybe that was the connection. "What happened to the second church on this site?"

"It was eventually moved to a farm, but I understand it's no longer there. This one was built in eighteen fifty."

"Thanks for your help." I turned to walk away, then spun back around. "Did you—or do you have to be—a member of St. Peter's church to be buried here?"

Rubbing his head like a genie lamp, he pondered. "I believe that has always been the case. If there was an exception, or two—" He chuckled as if privy to a private joke. "Addison would be the one to ask."

"Addison?" I heard the door open behind me, and the light poured down the aisle between the pews.

"He's our resident expert on the cemetery. I can get you his number if you like." He glanced over my head. "Welcome, folks. Come on in."

"Thanks. That would be great. I need to run to work, but I'll stop by tomorrow."

He'd moved past me as I was saying this to a very distinguished-looking middle-aged couple. "Welcome to St. Peter's. How can I help?"

*   *   *

Livia was at the bar wearing a T-shirt of a swearing chicken with the caption, Fluent in Fowl Language.

I stopped in my tracks as I realized she was wearing lipstick. "Oh. My. God. This is getting serious."

She'd been chatting with Chef who returned to the kitchen just as I was coming into the bar area. He gave me a mischievous grin and lightly punched my shoulder as he strolled by.

Livia patted her hair coquettishly. "Whatever do you mean?"

Crossing my arms, I said, "Lipstick? I can't remember if that's ever happened."

She actually giggled. It was charming and I realized that I, too, wanted this. Had been looking at it with my face pressed against the window, when I just needed to open the door and step inside.

"Ha. I'm just having a good time and realizing that I need a little more balance in my life. Something you might consider." She wagged a finger in my face. "I haven't seen Niko in the bar lately, and you look like you're not sleeping. What's going on?"

"Oh, no, you don't. I want to hear more about you and George." And I truly did, even more than I wanted to talk about my life.

There was a new energy to her that I envied. Being loved is a powerful thing. As she gushed about some of their adventures, I found my mind wandering. "Do you believe in ghosts?" I asked, while straightening the bar stools.

"Absolutely," Livia replied, pulling her buzzing phone from her pocket. She smiled and quickly tapped a response. "You can't possibly embrace the history of this place and not be a believer. We're one of the most haunted towns in all of Delaware." She beamed with delight saying this. "But that's what happens in a four-hundred-year-old city."

I began checking the stock, making notes of what I'd need to pull from the storeroom.

"What about you? Do you believe in ghosts?" she asked, making a quick note on her ever-present clipboard.

"Ummm... yeah. I kinda do." If she only knew.

"Are you back applying to medical schools? I know when you're this fastidious, you're grappling with something."

I stopped abruptly, realizing I was once again wiping down a very clean bar top. Why was I fighting the things I truly loved? *Surrender, Dorothy.*

"While I appreciate your efforts, you know you can always talk to me." She put her head between me and the bar and made me laugh.

At work, Livia was very rarely fun and games, and I was delighted to see this playfulness. My mind flashed back to sitting at Lewes Oyster Bar and my date with Niko. A delightful man who loved food and understood my passion for it. Double the fun.

"I know I can talk to you. And I hate sounding like a broken record. And yes, I know my dad would want me to be happy, yet I can't help but feel I need to honor his tradition of medicine. He helped so many people. Made a difference in so many lives. Owning a restaurant doesn't do that." Realizing what I said and to whom I said it, I put my hand over my mouth. "Liv—I'm so sorry—I didn't mean—"

Uncharacteristically Livia put her head back and really laughed. "First off, that's the only time I've heard you say 'own' a restaurant and that delights me. And of course you didn't offend me. I stopped caring what people thought when I hit fifty. At the end of the day, I love what I do, and so should you. I'd rather leave a legacy of joy than 'should' on myself. I 'should' do this, I 'should' do that. Doesn't turn out well. Trust me, I know." And she spun and headed towards the kitchen.

Hmmm. I did say 'own', didn't I?

36

〜

Niko hadn't come over Sunday night as he was working on a presentation for a potential investor. I found myself still pouting about it at the beach early the next morning, trying to decide whether or not I wanted to join the eight a.m. yoga class. It was a cloudy day which perfectly matched my mood. Then I felt a presence beside me. "Hello, Henry," I said, without even turning my head.

"Miss Vie," he chuckled. "Good morning to you."

I turned sideways to face him. He was in his ice sculpture form which I'd finally gotten used to, but none of that mattered. I was just happy to see him. It didn't matter *why* he was in my life. His presence was a gift and I loved it.

"Henry, how'd you like to go for a ride in my car?"

His face registered shock, then delight. "Oh, Miss Vie. Do you think that's even possible?" He turned and looked at my car parked just behind me. "I would, I would um, I would love that," he said, grinning.

It hadn't been my plan to drive to the beach. I often biked or jogged, but at the last minute I remembered I needed a few things from the store, so I'd driven. Not sure what prompted the offer of a ride. I was over being in my own head and I'd discovered the quickest way out of that was to do something for someone else.

"Who knows? Let's give it a shot." I stood, walked back to my car, and opened the passenger door. "Do I even need to do this? Or can you slide through metal?"

"I can," he said, then vibrated a moment as though he were shivering. "I can walk through anything if I'm in this form—but I don't enjoy the sensation. And I feel like if I just walk through a wall into someone's house, I'm invading their privacy. It's not in my nature."

Henry eased himself very slowly into my car. I laughed as I thought to tell him to buckle up, and he glanced up at me.

"I was thinking of telling you to put your seat belt on, and it made me laugh. I imagine it would pass right through you." Plus, you're already dead, I thought, but I wasn't about to remind him. "You mentioned some geographical boundaries? Remind me what happens when you go beyond those limits?" There was something novel and mischievous about the idea of racing around Lewes with a ghost in my car.

"It feels as though I suddenly go to sleep. And then I end up back in the cemetery sometime later. Might be a day or a week. My concept of time, as I think I may have told you, is rather murky. Forgive me if I repeat myself." He was gazing thoughtfully at everything on the dashboard, his eyes wide with wonder. "May I ask, what is this?" He pointed to the navigation screen. I tried to explain the screen, the backup camera, the radio, the speedometer. All of it. He was fascinated, I could tell, but I was eager to get on the road.

I chose a radio station with dance music and started bopping around in my seat. Henry seemed alarmed by this, so I turned it off.

"Would you mind," he asked, "if we just listened to the wind while you pilot this wonder?"

"No problem, Henry. No problem." Backing out slowly, I watched as he put his one hand on the dash, and the other on the console between us.

"It's ok, Henry. I promise not to go too fast."

"Oh, but you must, Miss Vie, you must."

I laughed. "Alrighty then. Let's do this!" We turned left at the Dairy Queen onto Cape Henlopen Drive. Just past East of Maui surf shop, I turned right and hit the gas. By the time I crossed the bridge over the canal, I was doing fifty. I was trying to remember his geographical boundaries as I didn't want him to disappear before we had our ride, when I heard this weird noise, almost like "Heeeeeeeeeeeeeeee." It was Henry. He had such an expression of absolute joy on his face, it made me want to cry.

Reaching over to pat his leg, I thought better of it. "Are you ok?"

He turned his head ever so slowly as though he was afraid to move, nodded once, then turned back to face forward, his eyes wide.

I slowed down and made the turn onto Monroe, so we could swing past the caboose at the Lewes Library. Pulling into the parking lot, I turned off the car and faced him. "Whaddya think?" I asked, grinning.

He closed his eyes and smiled. Then turned to me. "I... I have no words. It was just—" he put his hands in the air, then shrugged. "Magnificent. Beyond anything I could have imagined. I can't thank—" Then he was gone.

I leaned back in my seat and hugged myself. Even though he couldn't help leaving, it still stung. How was it possible to open oneself to love again with so much leaving?

I drove quickly to the cemetery to see if he was there, as that was where he always 'woke.' There was no sign of him anywhere. I got back in my Jeep and let the sadness wash over me.

37

After the cemetery, I was on my way to Lloyd's, the local market, for some essentials when my car decided to redirect itself to the Station. Why not have an amazing latte and that divine mushroom quiche? *Good idea, Stewart.*

I ordered and sat, and just as my food arrived, a tall, beautiful man sat down across from me.

"You can run, but you can't hide," Niko's velvety voice purred. His lovely hands reached across the table to mine.

Who's hiding, I thought. You were the one who blew me off. I tucked my hands back under the table.

Niko frowned. "Are we ok? I'm sorry I couldn't come over last night. I had the meeting this morning, then came here to grab a coffee when I saw you."

"I'm sorry. Life is just—a little weird at the moment." I brought my hands out and across the table to his.

He gave my hands a squeeze, kissed one, then sat back in his chair and crossed his arms. "I can do weird." He smiled and cocked his head.

Can you? I thought. *I just gave a ghost a ride in my car, how's that for starters*?

Niko studied my face, patiently waiting for me to continue. I deflected. "How'd your meeting go?"

His face fell somewhat which made me sad. Why couldn't I let him in? "I think it went well. They seemed really interested and made some worthwhile suggestions."

"Cool." *You're so weird, Stewart. Why are you blowing it*? What the hell, I thought. Taking a deep breath, I said, "Do you believe in ghosts?" If Niko truly cared, he needed to see all of me. Hot, goopy mess that I was. Waiting for his response I began pushing my quiche around my plate with my fork, picking at it, but not eating it.

"I don't not believe. I think there's a lot out there that we don't understand." One of the staff brought him a latte with a heart design on top, gave him a huge smile and wagged her fingers at him as she left. He leaned forward and wrapped his hands around the cup. "What do you think?"

I think that server is definitely interested. "Well, I hadn't thought much about it until my dad died. But I'd like to believe he's still part of my life or watching over me. I'd like to think if I passed, I could still keep an eye on Finn." I gave a half smile, missing my little bro. Then my thoughts returned to Henry. "But recently, I met a real ghost. I mean, I guess that's what you'd call him. Or a spirit. Or—" I looked up to see a puzzled look in Niko's eyes.

"You met?"

I tried desperately to read his face. Was that scorn? Skepticism? Concern? Not sure. But I plowed forward. "Yup. In

front of the Zwaanendael Museum. He was sitting on a bench."
I realized how bizarre this sounded. "No one had been able to
see him in over a hundred years. Then he just disappeared. But
we've met up again since, and I'm helping him find out what
happened to his family."

"You met a ghost on a bench."

I nodded.

"Should I be worried?" Niko once again reached for my
hand.

I put my hands back in my lap. "I can't tell you what to do."
As expected, this was not going well.

"No, I mean, is he frightening you?" He let his hand lie on
the table.

That was unexpected. "No—he's not scary at all. He's
actually lovely. Reminds me of my father." As soon as I said that,
I thought Niko would think my mind was playing games with
my grief, and I'd conjured up a ghost dad.

Niko sipped his latte and looked at his phone. "I don't have
to be anywhere till noon. Tell me more."

When he looked at the time, I'd immediately assumed he
was dismissing me. I realized then that I was interpreting every
look, every gesture, and everything that he said—or didn't—as
not believing me. But what if I was wrong?

"Well... his name is Henry. Actually, Robert Henry Edward
Talbot, but he goes by Henry, and his wife was pregnant when
he died, and he doesn't know what happened to her or the
baby or his two older sons. Oh, Niko." *Please don't think I'm
crazy.* "I can see him and hear him, but I don't think anyone else
can. He sometimes looks as solid as you or me, but sometimes

he looks more like an ice sculpture, and I can see through him. I'm working with a genealogist to trace his family, but she's not having much luck." I stopped to push my demolished, yet uneaten quiche to the side of the plate.

"I believe you. At least, I believe you think this is real."

I leaned back. He thought I was a head case. *Please, believe me.*

"That didn't come out right. I don't think you're making this up. It's very real to you. But it's hard to wrap my head around something I haven't personally experienced. Especially something that sounds other worldly."

"You think I'm nuts." I spat out the words.

"No, Vie, no. Greeks are very superstitious. My great grandmother had all kinds of stories that made my hair stand on end. I haven't personally experienced anything of a supernatural nature, but it doesn't mean it doesn't exist." He ran his fingers through his hair. "Here's what I know. I think you're incredible. I love how kind and caring you are. I love your curiosity about life and food and everything in general. I love that I am totally myself around you and I like who I am around you. And if that means I have a girlfriend who believes in ghosts, I'm good with that."

Girlfriend. Wait. What? "Girlfriend?"

"I'd love for you to be my girlfriend. If that's what *you* want."

I was so afraid of saying something stupid at this point, I just nodded. I didn't want to cry.

Niko smiled. "Yes, that's what you want? Yes, you'll be my girlfriend?"

My head continued bobbing while my mind raced. Oh, God, I wanted this. I did. I do. But what now? What if I fuck this up? Just say yes, Stewart. Say YES. And we'll sort the rest out later.

"Yes," I said. "Yes."

38

I woke up on a Tuesday morning with a luscious man curled around me. "Oh good, you're awake," he said, spinning me towards him. He then proceeded to cover my face, neck and shoulders with kisses before leaping out of bed. "I'm starving. Hope you're hungry." And off he went.

Lying on my back, I looked up at the ceiling and decided this was a very good way to start the day. Niko had picked me up and taken me back to his place, a condo in an old church on Mulberry Street in downtown Lewes. He was renting from a friend, so it was hard to tell what were his touches on the place as opposed to the owner's.

As he walked around shirtless in blue drawstring pants, I studied his tattoos. His back was completely covered with the most stunning array of fruits and veggies, interwoven with greens and vines that gave it almost a jungle feel. There was also a large chef's knife as part of the tableau and smaller kitchen accoutrements like a whisk, a spoon, and a pepper mill. His right upper arm and chest was covered with the Greek god, Poseidon, his trident, and an assortment of sea creatures surrounded by crashing waves. All of them truly works of art.

"So, let's get back to your ghost," Niko said, pulling pans from a drawer.

"Ok. Whaddya wanna know?" And what was I willing to tell?

"Why do you think you're the only one who can see and hear him?"

A question I asked myself daily. What *was* our connection? Is it my dad? He and Henry were so alike. But I didn't know. I really didn't. "I haven't a clue. He said it hasn't happened for a hundred years. It was a woman before as well, but she was so frightened, he said, they never really engaged." Watching Niko cook was an aphrodisiac. Seriously. Chopping scallions, cracking eggs, whisking, whatever. It was a joy to watch. "You're incredible."

"What?" He turned to me laughing, as he effortlessly flipped the omelet.

"No, really. Watching you—it's like watching someone conduct a symphony. Or a dancer float across the stage. You were born to do this."

He bowed before me. "I appreciate the compliment. It gives me great joy to cook for others."

The smells. Oh the smells. Mushrooms in sherry with fresh rosemary. If my nose could swoon, it would. "If you—no, WHEN—you open your restaurant, you need to have a counter where people can watch you cook. Or a chef's table at least."

"That's an interesting idea. I just don't want to do what everyone else is doing, but I also don't want to be different, just to be different, you know?"

I nodded with a huge smile on my face. "Exactly." I casually opened drawers and peeked in his cupboards, looking for spices and what else he kept in his pantry.

"I want to do Mediterranean, but with a twist. Not fusion, God I hate that word."

Laughing, I said, "You *do*? You used it the first time you talked about your restaurant. Made me worry." I leaned against the counter.

"You're right, I remember. As soon as I said it, I cringed inside. Forgive me. I really do know what kind of food I want to serve." Niko turned off the stove. Placing the plates on the counter in front of me, he fed me the first bite.

"That's a relief." I laughed, then took a bite. "Jesus, Niko. This should be illegal. It's sooo good. What the sherry does to the mushrooms, and what else is that, thyme?"

"Feeding you is fun, you know that, right?"

"Everything with me is fun; don't you think?" Laughing, I devoured every last crumb on my plate.

"Can we get back to your ghost? Or did you think that complimenting me was an excellent way to change the subject?"

"Nope. I'm trying to think about what I haven't told you. I chased after him once and when I touched him my hand went through him like he was Jell-O. Freaked me out, a bit." *And my knees buckled, and I went down.*

"Jell-O? Ohmigod. Wait. Maybe I could feel him, even though I can't see or hear him."

Why is that important? I wondered. "Possibly. I have no idea."

"Your body language just changed. I don't need to meet him or touch him. I just want you to know that I'm happy to share in as much or as little of this as you want me to."

Damned perceptive chef man. Swirling my coffee, I was quiet. Was I ready to share Henry? Why the defensive knee jerk reaction to Niko meeting him? Who was I protecting? Henry? Me?

"I think it's cool you've met a ghost." He shook his head. "I'm sorry. That sounded patronizing, as though you were a child with an imaginary friend. The truth is, the more I thought about your Henry, the more amazing I thought it was. I loved that he chose you. How could he not?"

I looked at Niko. *What a wonderful thing for you to say.* "Thank you. I love that I can see him, that he can see me, and we connected. When I'm with him, I'm reminded of how special I felt being with my father. Henry's a gift to me as much as I am to him." I gathered our dishes and put them in the sink, giving myself a moment to regroup. Niko was being sweetly curious and kind, and I needed to take a breath and allow myself to accept that. Not my default setting for sure. *Assume the best, Stewart, not the worst.*

"What's all this?" I tried to change the subject by pointing to the spread of cookbooks, papers, drawings, all over the dining room table.

"I know what you're doing, and it's ok. Whenever you want to talk more about Henry, I'm here." As he walked behind me, he kissed me on the shoulder. "This is floor plans for the restaurant, notes for investors, recipes, and mail I haven't opened in weeks. There's so much to this business. I knew but didn't know."

I gazed at recipe after recipe with notations in the margins, food stains, and things scratched out. Some looked really old. I picked up one in handwriting that looked like the author had trouble holding the pencil. I could barely read it.

"My Ya-Ya, my mother's mother, tried to write her recipe for spanakopita in English for me." He smiled. "Of course, my mother thinks her version is better even though they're almost exactly the same. Food is a competitive sport in our family."

"I love that," I said, running my fingers over the handwriting. "I think you said Ya-Ya taught you to cook?"

"Yes, we spent a lot of time together while my mother worked."

I started reading through the ingredients of spinach, feta, eggs, onion, and garlic, tasting the flavors together in my mind. "Would you change the recipe for the restaurant?"

"Maybe. I like making small tweaks. Keep the original gist of the dish, but maybe add mushrooms, or a second type of cheese. My Ya-Ya preferred halloumi and my mother used feta. Feta is drier and crumblier, but they're both salty and cheesy."

"Do you have a name yet? I still like Olive."

"Seventeen last I counted. I keep adding to the list, then crossing one off, and so on."

"What? Why so many?"

"The naming is hard. So hard. It conjures an image, and I'm still refining the menu. One of my friends said Niko's sounds like an Italian take out. I also think the location will contribute to the name."

"Do you have a spot in mind?" *Please be Lewes or someplace close.*

Grinning like a Cheshire cat, he nodded. "I do."

"Tell me." I tapped a finger on his chest.

Taking a deep breath, he took his hand in mine. "I wouldn't offer pub food, so we wouldn't be competing, but I'm talking to the owner of the space between Biblion Books and the liquor store."

"That's almost across the street from the pub! But we could handle the competition." I put my hands on my hips. Besides. More downtown Lewes restaurants would bring more tourists. Anything but more real estate offices. "Are you thinking casual or fine?"

"I'd like to walk the line, but then we run into the 'fusion' issue again."

We both laughed.

"So, probably fine dining in a more casual atmosphere. Because I'm going to be tweaking some traditional dishes, I think I need to attract a more sophisticated palate. Does that make sense?"

"Absolutely." I was running different flavor scenarios in my mind in regards to spanakopita.

Placing his hands on either side of my head, he kissed the top of it, then rested his forehead against mine. "What's running through that brilliant mind of yours?"

"It's nothing. Just playing with tastes and stuff."

"Like... C'mon share. I love your palate."

"What if you did spanakopita egg rolls?"

"I love that idea." He clapped his hands together. "What else?"

"I love phyllo pastry, and I can think of dozens of fillings that would be fun—like a mushroom based one, since you brought that up."

"See that sounds fun and a little unexpected, which I like. I once had a deconstructed strawberry shortcake, that was so far from the original dish that it felt more like art than food. That just doesn't work for me."

"So... nods to your Greek heritage, but not strictly a Mediterranean restaurant?" I grabbed a pen from the counter and pretended to make notes on my hand.

"Yes. I think so. But what do you think? What type of restaurant do you think Lewes needs, or what would you open?"

I glowed from his interest. It was so wonderful to be seen and acknowledged for my passion with food.

"Vie? I feel like I lost you there."

"Oh, sorry. Why not consider your place American cuisine with Mediterranean influences?"

He snorted. "I think my Ya-Ya just slapped the back of my head, but yes, I think you may be right, my wise one."

We talked food a moment longer, then I excused myself to go sketch and get ready for work. I was grateful the conversation hadn't circled back to Henry. Seems I was more protective than I thought.

39

Instead of doing any of the things I had planned, I found myself standing in St. Peter's cemetery. FindAGrave.com had a list of every single person buried here, but none of the last names matched Henry's. Yet he kept returning here, and not of his own volition. Why?

According to FindAGrave, there were twenty-six women named Sarah buried in this cemetery. But from what I could tell, none of them were her: different middle names and none born in 1777.

Neither of his sons was buried here either. But the unborn child, the son or perhaps the daughter might have been. I texted and left messages for my genealogist who promised to get back to me shortly.

Doing all this poking and probing of the past made me curious about my own lineage. Not my dad's side—he'd traced his Scottish roots way back. But my mother, that was a different story. Both her parents, Evelyn and Peter, had died before I was born. My mother didn't talk much about them; apparently her mother had not been a very loving or affectionate woman. Come to think about it, my mom wasn't the warm fuzzy person in my family either. It had always been my dad.

"Hey daddy. I'm back in the graveyard again." I'd been talking to him more often. I felt more connected after spending time with Henry. He wasn't buried here; his ashes had been scattered at sea per his request. "I'm not getting very far very fast with my search for Henry, but I like being around him. He reminds me of you." I hugged myself, suddenly feeling a chill.

"I consider that a huge compliment, Miss Vie." Henry stood beside me, looking every bit like a normal human being. Same clothes, never the worse for wear—cream blouse, gray pants, wool vest. I didn't realize he was taller than I was as most of our encounters he'd been seated.

"Henry. Wow. You're so... so solid."

He chuckled slightly. "Am I? I have no idea how or why, either. How are you, my dear?"

"Happy that we met. If I hadn't told you that before, I want you to know."

Henry beamed.

"And you liked riding in the car, I could tell."

"Oh my, yes. That was... that was... indescribable. Thank you again. I only wish I could do something for you in return."

"Tell my dad I love him. And I miss him."

"I wish that I could." He shook his head. "I have actually talked to many graves in many cemeteries, trying to see if I could communicate with those that had passed."

"Really? Did you ever sense anyone trying to talk back?"

"Sadly, no. At times I thought that maybe there were others in a state like myself, so I've said hello to hundreds of strangers over the years, but to no avail. I can't tell you my excitement and utter joy when you could not only hear me but see me. That is the true gift you have given me, Miss Vie."

We stared at the tombstones, each one representing a life lived. Both of us seemed comfortable with the silence. A breeze ruffled the leaves in the tree closest to us and I closed my eyes as it teased my hair. "Henry, if you had to guess where you were buried, where do you think it is?"

"Only wealthier folks would have been buried in a church cemetery. Unknown sailors were buried near the water. But if I had to guess, I'm most likely on my land, which is no longer my land. My grave might have been marked with a stone, or a wooden cross."

I thought about the historical marker that reads "Unknown Sailors' Cemetery" at the Cape May Lewes Ferry. Over 800 'souls' lost at sea over the years had washed up near that location, many of those unidentified buried where the parking lot was now. According to paranormal investigators, the Ferry Terminal was definitely haunted.

Haunted. What did I know about haunting and ghosts anyway? Henry had challenged all of that for me. I had always pictured white translucent things that were kind of there, but not there. Or a glimpse of something out of the corner of your eye; like you saw something, but did you really? Then movies like Ghostbusters where there were, of course, white wispy women who turned into something terrifying, or green goo that dripped from the ceiling. Then there was Nearly Headless Nick in Harry Potter—again a white, semi-transparent being.

I had Googled 'pictures of ghosts' and everything I found looked Photoshopped to me. I'd also seen photos taken by friends with a white orb somewhere in the picture, which people claimed were spirits. I'd snapped several photos of Henry surreptitiously (at least, I thought I was being clever till one day he asked if any of the daguerreotypes had actually shown an image of him). They hadn't.

His family had lived and died before photography was a thing, so I knew there weren't photos to be found. "What was the name of the last woman who saw you? Do you remember?"

"I do not. Unfortunately, I frightened her so much, I never saw her again. It was as though *she* disappeared."

"Are we ghost hunting?"

A familiar voice came from over my left shoulder.

I turned to see Paris in a ruby red tuxedo jacket with a matching full length fitted skirt and ruby red sequined heels. "You look ravishing. What's the occasion, Dorothy?"

Paris threw his head back and laughed.

I glanced to see if Henry was still there, and was delighted to find that he was. He had faded to more of the iceman state and his eyes were very round as he took in my larger-than-life friend.

"Girl, what are you doing in this graveyard, anyway?" Paris sucked in a breath. "Oooh! Oooh! Is Henry here?" He did a 360 in those heels, which sparkled in the sun.

I could feel my nostrils flare. "Yessss. As a matter of fact, he is." I nodded to my right.

"Where? Show me."

"An arm's length to my right." I was almost afraid to move. It was the first time anyone I knew had been this close to Henry.

"Miss Vie. Is this man, um woman, um, is this a friend of yours?" Henry stammered, but in a very kind tone.

"Yes. Henry meet Paris. Paris meet Henry."

"Dee-lighted to meet you at last," Paris said, stepping in front of me and moving closer.

"My pleasure," said Henry, nodding to Paris.

Henry could see Paris, but Paris couldn't see Henry and was talking to the space between us.

Paris whispered to me out of the side of his mouth, "What's he saying?"

"Pleasure to meet you." I responded. And he's not sure if you are a man or a woman, I wanted to say, which Paris wouldn't have minded, but would have mortified Henry, the epitome of politeness.

"Ohmigosh this is exciting. Henry, I really am a huge fan. Vie has told me so much about you. I hope we can find your family. Vie is trying, you know. She's awesome, by the way, but I guess you already know that."

"Are you done?" I asked, turning to Paris. Henry was still staring, then he'd catch himself and look away.

I giggled to myself.

Hand on hip, Paris turned to me. "Why are you laughing?"

"I think Henry is not sure…" I hesitated. Again, I think poor Henry would be mortified if I actually said this out loud.

"Oh. OH." Paris turned towards the vicinity of Henry again. "Dear sir. I am a man, who sometimes dresses like a woman. And again, I am so pleased to meet you." Turning back to me, Paris continued, "Can you ask him if he can see anyone around me. Spirit like?"

Henry was shaking his head. Eyes wide.

"Dorothy—he can hear you. You just can't hear him. And he says no. In fact, I don't think he's ever seen another spirit. At least, that he knows of."

"Well then. Unfortunately, I can't stay and chat. I peeked in the bar, and you weren't there, then I saw you here. I gotta go prep for a Barbie party, for which I will need you and at least one pink drink. I'll text you details. Toodles." And with a little wave he sashayed away.

My heart felt unexpectedly full. Paris, being his fabulous, warm, and wonderful self, had taken the meeting in stride like he met a ghost on a daily basis. Henry had now met Paris. Paris cared. Henry cared. I was seen and I was loved and I was ever so grateful for it.

40

During my senior year in high school, my dad had collected course catalogs from all over the Eastern seaboard. Hopkins, Duke, Harvard, Yale. He was convinced I could go anywhere I liked, or at least, he gave that impression. I knew from research how slim my chances were. Harvard received 8000 applications for 220 openings. Daunting, to say the least. We'd finally agreed that the University of Delaware, just ninety miles from home, would be fine to get some undergrad credits out of the way. Then I could come home on weekends, if I wanted.

I remember him being so excited that I was really going to follow in his path. He never looked at it as a given, but rather an unexpected gift.

Henry was also an unexpected gift. I realized through him, I was remembering more of my dad, mourning my dad, and letting go of some of the pain and grief.

I'd kept the brochures. They were in a battered suitcase under my bed that I'd brought with me when I moved into the carriage house. It was a small, tired, brown thing with tiny brass clips that made a satisfying clack when closed. Covered in stickers from faraway places, it had been Dad's when he was younger, and his dad's before that. Over the years I'd added childhood stickers of my own.

I poured myself a glass of wine, pulled the suitcase out, and sat on the floor with my back to the sofa. It was pouring outside and I paused and listened to the rain pound away on the roof and the skylight. Taking a deep breath, I opened the case. Inside were things that were precious to me. A tie I'd given him when I was five with cartoon sailboats on it. He'd worn it often. His first stethoscope. A name tag with Dr. Alexander Stewart on it. Ticket stubs from the movie *Master and Commander*—we'd gone twice. For him, it was anything to do with the sea. My dad loved pointing out nautical terms that people used in everyday language. "Feeling blue," came from when a captain or officer of a ship died at sea and the crew would fly blue flags and paint a blue band along the ship's hull.

For me, that movie was the start of a fascination with history and seafaring traditions. I still loved learning the why of things. Like the term "square meal." It was a nautical term from the days of old sailing ships. Any significant meals would be eaten off a square-shaped wooden plate that also served as the tray.

Gathering up the brochures, I held them close to my chest, knowing he'd gathered them for me. "I love you, daddy. I miss you." My throat tightened. The rain continued to drum the roof.

Going back to med school would have made him proud, yes, but my passion had moved on. To food. To all the flavors that create a dish. To square meals. To running the front of house. Making patrons feel like there was no place they'd rather be.

Consistently good food and good service at a reasonable cost. It felt like a dance and it gave me absolute joy. *That* was what I knew my dad would have wanted for me.

Logan, hadn't a clue about who he was. Or what made him happy. His father had put him on the family conveyor belt, and expected him to never step off, never detour, never question the path they'd laid out for him. Maybe that's why I was thinking about him now. My life, too, had been on a track. Goals in mind. Everything planned out.

I pictured my dad standing in front of me right now. If I asked him what he wanted me to be when I grew up, I knew for sure what he would have said.

Happy.

41

Livia positively glowed.

"Oh, God. You're in love, aren't you? If I didn't know better, I'd think you were pregnant."

She giggled.

"Did you just giggle? Just stop. You're nauseating the staff." I'd come in early to do some kitchen inventory and meet the repair guy who was investigating an oven burner that had been misbehaving. Livia was there doing payroll.

"I can't remember ever feeling like this. Not with any man I've been with." She leaned back in her office chair. "It's almost magical. I have to pinch myself sometimes, because it doesn't feel real. And to think. That man has been sitting at my bar for years. Who knew?" Livia ran her finger around the handle on her coffee cup, then headed to the bar area.

"Well, I'm very happy for you. And maybe—" I pinched my fingers together. "A little jealous."

"You? YOU? What about that Greek god that comes in more often than ever? The one you talk food with while the rest of us yell 'get a room.'"

I felt the blood rush to my face. "What? That's...that's... just silly." I straightened the chairs next to the bar.

Livia laughed heartily. "You're not fooling anyone, Genevieve Stewart. Especially me." She put a hand on my arm. "It's wonderful. Embrace it. Don't overthink it. He doesn't have to be Mr. Right. Let him be Mr. Right Now. You're having fun and it shows."

Deflecting, I retorted, "You're one to talk. What's next? A wedding in Bora Bora?" I crossed my arms, removing myself from her touch.

"Ummm... I was thinking more like the new Viking cruise that goes to Antarctica," she said, in the same tone as 'pass the salt.'

"Ohmigod are you serious? You're getting married?"

"Don't be ridiculous." Then she looked thoughtful. "Unless the tax ramifications are more favorable. I may have to look into that." She tapped her lip.

"Stop messing with me. What is going on?"

"I'm not getting married. But I really like our Walrus. And it's fun traveling with him. Having you here makes me feel like everything will be ok. You're the most responsible person I know, and it makes me proud watching you run the place." She gave me a look of utter and complete love. "You're the daughter I never had."

Without thinking, I threw myself at her and she hugged me like there was no tomorrow. Then she put me at arm's length so she could see my face. "You of all people know that life is short. We all deserve to be happy. To be loved. By people who genuinely care about us."

Nodding with tears in my eyes, I found I couldn't speak.

"So, I really do want to take that Antarctic trip. I'm going to take six weeks and go away. You've got this."

"Of course," I said without hesitation. But *ohmigod* ran through my mind.

*　　*　　*

When I woke in the middle of the night there was no way I was going back to sleep. Holy shit. I'd be on my own running Grace's. No Livia safety net. What if chef quit? Or another outbreak of Covid? Or a customer drank too much and we got sued? Or shut down? Dear god. My mind ran amok.

Being handed the responsibility of the bar cemented my decision not to carry on the medical profession in our family. I didn't want it anymore. I'd like to pretend it was that easy. Just say no to becoming a doctor. But the guilt was there and maybe always would be.

I got up and made myself a cup of tea. Grace O'Malley's would be mine for six weeks. Scary, but cool. I wanted it, to be honest. I knew I had what it took to run the place and now I'd been given the opportunity to prove it. What wasn't working? What could be done better? Theme nights seemed to do well in bars—could we do another? Our Lewes History trivia night was amazing with the people and revenue it brought in.

What about brunch? Guest chefs? Special events—ooh—definitely needed to pick Paris' brain on this. Look at me, I thought. Look how excited I am! *Hello Stewart—this is the life you love and want.* I did a happy dance around the room.

What about a cool logo and some merch? Our website could use a bit of a makeover. I laughed out loud. Livia would return and find she'd created a monster.

42

I have news—I texted my boys, Paris and Niko. *Can we meet at the Library later tonight?*

Both said they'd be there around ten.

Should I be surprised at how excited I was? I'd thought of nothing else since Livia told me and I'd barely slept. She hadn't asked me to makeover her restaurant, but I couldn't stop thinking about all the things I'd do differently. Definitely more social media for a younger crowd. Then would we stay open later? Lewes was notorious for rolling up the sidewalks rather early. And nobody tipped or drank like my gay boys. Was there a way of making it more welcoming for them?

Could I make Niko a guest chef? Would Cleveland, our chef, be cool with that? He could take an extra night off, then, if he liked. But for our regulars, how would they feel walking through the door and finding Mediterranean on the menu?

What I found so interesting about this was that I had more questions than answers despite having worked at Grace's for five years. I'd never questioned Cleveland about the menu; I'd just assumed he and Livia collaborated on it and what we had was what they came up with. Was he really happy there? And able to cook the food he loved?

I was still in my twitchy state when I arrived at Grace's, so I was even more anal in setting up for the evening, lining all the bar chairs up like little soldiers, and rearranging the liquor bottles. When Livia caught me turning each bottle, so the label faced perfectly forward, she put a hand on my arm. "You're going to be great."

"I'll be fine." I said, not really meeting her eyes. Then I spotted Henry in the cemetery. Shit. "Gimme a sec. Gotta grab something from the walk-in."

Practically running through the kitchen, I sprinted out the rear door and over to the church entrance. "Pssst. Henry! Over here." The last thing I needed was for Liv to see me talking to apparently no one. She'd not only leave someone else in charge, but she might have me committed.

Henry turned, gave me a wave and a smile, and headed over. "Why, Miss Vie. Good afternoon." Then he frowned. "What's happened? You look pale."

"Henry, you have no idea. It occurred to me that I could check church records! They often recorded births, marriages, and deaths, and I wanted to find out when you were a member here?" I nodded towards St. Peter's.

"I wasn't." He looked puzzled.

"Oh. I thought for sure you were since you kept showing up here." *Stewart, calm down.* I took a breath. "What about Sarah? Was she a member here?"

"Now I see the line of your inquiry." Henry began pacing. "Sarah's family were members here, and we'd attend on occasion.

But, Miss Vie, I rarely came. It was a matter of discord between myself and my lovely wife. And the memory of it now pains me, as she's gone, but there you have it."

"Oh. Oh!" I hadn't meant to upset him. "I'm so sorry. I have to go back to work." I turned but then spun back. "I'm going to be running the bar for the next several weeks while my boss travels, so my time will be limited. But I will keep searching, I promise. And I'll come say hello whenever I can."

"Of course. That sounds like a tremendous vote of confidence in your abilities. I hope—" Henry got a puzzled look as his form wavered, then turned to a million tiny black spots and disappeared.

I gasped. This had never happened before. I stared at the space where Henry had been. What the hell? Something had changed, but what? Was he ok? It left me with an uneasy feeling as I crossed the street and went back to work. Although we were super busy, I couldn't stop thinking about him. He'd never disappeared in this fashion and I hoped it didn't mean his time was coming to an end. No. No. No. I couldn't shake this sense of impending doom.

Heading to the Library after close, I discovered my boys were already there. There was a new bartender I didn't recognize. Guy with a chestnut man bun, late twenties with a tight black shirt that showed off his physique.

Niko stood as I came over and kissed my cheek. "What can I get you to drink, my lady?"

Paris gave me a little wave. It had been a strange twenty-four hours, and I wasn't feeling at all myself. Between my worry about handling the bar without fucking things up and Henry's strange exit, I was anywhere but there. Frowning, Paris stared a moment, then nodded towards the bar. "Check out the new eye candy. The Library is the gift that keeps on giving." He leaned back and sipped his Cosmo.

"I don't know him either. Let me go introduce myself." Niko looked surprised but I needed a moment to regroup. Normally I had solid footing in the Library, always finding familiar faces. Tonight, I felt like I was on a boat, trying to find my sea legs. I hardly recognized anyone.

"What can I get you?" Man bun stood before me.

"Oh, um, I uh, lemme have..." I glanced around the bar but didn't have a clue. "How about a cab. Um, whatever you have by the glass."

"Gotcha." He pointed over my left shoulder. "Ready for a refill?"

I turned to see Niko behind me. "Yes, thanks," he said, and glanced at me. "Are you ok? You seem distracted."

I gazed up into those dark pools. Leaning into him I wrapped my arms around his waist. "Hi. Not really."

He kissed the top of my head, paid for my drink and led me back to a circle of comfy chairs and a low table. "Come. Tell us all about it."

"What's up, Vivalicious?" Paris leaned forward, resting his elbows on his knees. He was in an all-black suit with a sequined black collarless shirt, and shiny black loafers with no socks.

"I'm worried about Henry. I saw him at the church just before my shift and when he disappeared, it was ... different." I gulped half my drink. My knights glanced at each other. "And Livia is traveling for six weeks and leaving me in charge.

I'm already freaking out. I mean, I know I can handle it, it's just…a lot."

"Yeah, it is, but how exciting!" Niko reached over and squeezed my hand. "You've got this. But I hear your concern about Henry."

"Yes. Something's changing. Not sure what it means." *Oh, Henry. Please be ok. Please. I can't lose you too. I can't.*

Paris tipped back his glass and drained it. "Did your genie friend come up with any answers?"

"Genie friend?" Niko held out his hand for Paris' glass.

"Genealogist. I'll take a refill too, thanks." I handed Niko my glass and some cash.

"I got this," he said, and headed back to the bar.

We both watched Niko glide across the room. So did a number of other women, and a few men as well. "He's pretty, isn't he," I said. "Kind. Smart. Ambitious. Not sure I won't make him crazy before all is said and done."

"He adores you and you'll handle it. Just like you'll handle Grace O'Malley's. Livia knows this or you wouldn't be left in charge." Paris glanced at his phone which was lighting up. "Oh good. My honey bunny just arrived at the airport and will be home in two hours. Daddy gonna get some tonight."

"Thank you for sharing. Haven't seen you much in the bar and haven't gotten many calls to bartend for you. What's going on?"

"Oh, you know. Training new staff. Streamlining some things. Weighing the difference between buying and storing some standard props versus renting every time. I think chocolate fountains are passe, but the clients keep asking."

Niko returned with our drinks and sat opposite me. "What did I miss? What's up with Henry?"

I was grateful he asked. "Well, normally he disappears a certain way. It's hard to explain. It seems like keeping a more solid form requires energy, so after a time he fades to what I call his ice form, where I can kinda see through him, then from his ice form, he just, like, 'poof' disappears. One second there, then gone. But today was different."

"You saw him today? Where?" Niko was all in. I loved this. I loved how he cared. How they both cared.

"The cemetery. He ends up there a lot. Anytime he disappears, he always reappears in the same place."

"That's interesting. Do you think his wife or children are buried there?" Niko rested his hand on my leg and left it there.

"He doesn't recognize the names of anyone in the area he typically 'arrives' in. He knows who some of the people are who are buried there, but no family that he knows of." I ran my fingers through my hair.

"Yeah, but married names might be different." Niko studied me.

"But he had two boys. Maybe his wife was pregnant with a girl, but we don't know. So far, my genie hasn't found anything about him or his wife or sons."

We all sat quietly pondering this a moment while the volume in the bar increased. More of the local service staff arrived. Wick and Chef waved when we saw each other and the familiar faces helped me relax.

Niko and particularly Paris were great sounding boards for my ideas about Grace O'Malley's, and in the end I knew I would reign it in and perhaps float one or two thoughts out to Livia before she left. I didn't want her to worry, I knew I was the right woman for the job.

It was fun listening to Paris talk about the business side of his event planning. I was always caught up in the imaginative side of it, but the practicality of it was mind blowing. Especially the larger events which required almost military precision in the execution. Dinners for hundreds of people made my head spin. Niko agreed. They both emphasized that the right staff could make or break you.

Niko had an early appointment, so he kissed me goodnight and promised to call the next day. Once he left, Paris got a serious look on his face. "I know you're worried about Henry. Exactly how was his disappearance different today?" Paris slipped his phone back in his pocket.

"You know what a Seurat painting is? Well, some of his paintings. They look like they're made with tiny dots. It's called pointillism. Well, today Henry turned into a million black dots before he disappeared. It was like a Seurat painting." Funny how we equate darkness with death. I shuddered remembering. My poor Henry.

"What if he's dying? Tiny black dots do not sound good."

"Well, he's already dead, Paris."

"You know what I mean. What if his spirit time is coming to an end? We have got to find this man some answers."

43

Livia and I were sitting in the bar about an hour before we opened. Her shirt said, 'I would agree with you, but then we'd both be wrong'. I smiled. The clouds kept the sun from shining through the stained glass above the windows, so the bar felt monochromatic. Devoid of color, much like a black and white picture.

"What would you like me to do while you're gone?" I asked.

Livia looked at me like I had something strange protruding from my face. "Carry on. Put August in an Uber if he drinks too much, let Cleveland control the menu, don't fire anyone unless it's truly necessary," Livia paused, "Why? Are you having second thoughts?"

As usual, I was overthinking this. "Nope. No. I just wanted to make sure there wasn't anything else you needed while you were away."

Her eyes crinkled, and she put her hand out. "Show me the list."

"What list?" I could feel my nostrils flare. God, she was good.

"The list you've been compiling about what you'd do differently. I know you. It's on your phone. Have you even slept since I asked you?" Then she laughed. "You'll be fine, but you're going to show me that list."

Reluctantly I typed in my password and handed her the phone. I felt like a sixteen-year-old caught with condoms in my purse. Could this be any more embarrassing?

"Hmmm. Guest chef. Talk with Cleveland. Not sure how he'd feel about it, but he's mentioned something called 'Rock the Menu', where one night a month he really shakes things up in the kitchen."

"That's an awesome idea, I—" My face felt hotter by the minute. Maybe the bar had no color but my face surely did. Noises drifted through from the kitchen as more staff arrived. The music changed from James Taylor to The Rolling Stones.

Livia shook her head. "Chef is testing me." She returned to my list. "Social media. Not a bad idea, but twenty somethings don't spend as much as our usual clientele, and they don't tip for shit. But I do like the idea of expanding our marketing and Instagram and Facebook are an inexpensive way to do that." Livia nodded.

"Who are you and what have you done with Livia? Is this because you're in love?" I crossed my arms and gave her my most intimidating stare which I knew she could flick away like a fly.

"Ha! A little of that, yes. And Covid. And your dad. Our lives just don't go on forever, you know? Feeling my own mortality. I want to make sure I'm living my best life, not just working my ass off and crawling into bed every night. The more time I spend with George, the more I want to do. No regrets."

My thoughts jumped to my Dad. I knew there was so much more that he'd planned for his life. A safari. Taking his sailboat from Lewes to Bermuda. A river cruise down the Seine. We'd talked about running a clinic together. Just me and him. I think I was more like the firstborn son. Like my dad and I were cut from the same cloth. "I know what you mean. You mentioned Antarctica— is that where you'll go first?" Livia was still studying my phone. "Anything else while you're gone?"

"We have a good crew here. I think you'll be fine with staffing. Cleveland's only been out sick one time in all the years he's been here. And I know you have bartender friends if you need them. Are you good for trivia night? There's a folder in my office—I try to keep track of the questions and rotate them."

"What if we did some kind of bar crawl, or scavenger hunt, or history trail event thing that involved other restaurants or shops? Would you be good with that?" I was so pleased how Livia was responding to my list.

"That sounds like fun but would probably require a lot more than a month's planning. I'm thinking of the amount of time to get the word out and all that. But we're on good terms with everyone in town, so it might be kind of fun. A way to get some business in the doors of shops that people don't frequent as much."

My head was once again spinning with ideas. I loved this. I could eat it with a spoon. "What if I came up with a new logo and we started selling some merch?"

Livia's eyes narrowed. "Whaddya have in mind? Nothing too dark or silly. Don't want to disrespect my Grace, you know."

"Absolutely not. Let me just—" I reached for my phone and quickly found the one I liked the most—a skull and crossbones, except the skull had female shaped almond eyes, a jaunty hat and the crossbones were a knife and fork. "Maybe?" I asked, showing it to Livia.

"Ha! Clever. Your idea or Paris'?"

"Mine, thank you very much."

"Ok. Let me think about that." Livia handed me back my phone. "Good job, Stewart. You've got this."

44

I constantly worried about Henry. The black dot disappearance, like a doomsday pointillism painting, seemed ominous. What could it mean? What could any of this mean? I thought about contacting some of the paranormal investigators that I'd seen in Lewes over the years but wasn't ready to reveal my own private ghost. I feared they'd be too caught up in the fact that I could see and hear him to be of any help.

While it was easier to think of Henry as a ghost, my research had come up with a plethora of spirit related words including an *eidolon*, an *apparition*, a *phantom*, a *specter* (which seemed to describe him the best in that it meant an unnatural entity becoming visible), a *wraith*, a *wight*, a *poltergeist, revenant,* and a *banshee.* Even Henry had no idea what he was. My biggest resistance to calling him a ghost was that it conjured scary things, and Henry was not. But words in this list (other than ghost) felt creepy to me. And Casper had been friendly, right?

He could have been scary, I guess. I'd heard of things being moved in some of the older homes in town, like a workman's tools at the Cannonball house, but Henry claimed he couldn't move anything. He said he could pass through walls but preferred not to. No one else could see him or hear him. Wonder if they could feel him?

Black dots. Black dots. I Googled everything imaginable, 'does a ghost die?', or 'can a ghost change form?' but nothing helpful came up. Ditto for my search for "Reporting a ghost sighting." Most sites felt like the ramblings of people who needed to be on medication.

Niko was meeting with a number of potential investors and totally distracted most of the time we spent together, so I kept my Henry concerns to myself.

Time with my Adonis was mostly fabulous sex followed by a rock star breakfast. Fine for now because I, Genevieve Stewart, had a restaurant to run.

But in my heart of hearts, I felt Henry was running out of time.

Don't go, Henry. Don't go.

45

∽

"Cleveland. How would you feel about a guest chef?" I'd come in early to chat and ended up getting assigned the task of julienning carrots. But he also let me taste the black bean soup which surprised me with a hint of lemon. It amazed me how quickly his spotless, stainless domain quickly became organized chaos as staff prepped food for the evening's service.

"What's that mean?" He crossed his arms over his white double-breasted coat, which had felt too formal, I thought, for the kitchen of an Irish pub. But it did make a statement. It set him apart and was the traditional uniform of every high-end kitchen. He was the lord of this part of the house and I would be counting on him more than ever in the coming weeks.

"You know. Like on your night off if we had a guest chef in the kitchen, making something not on our menu."

"Here's my concern. Ninety nine percent of the time, people don't know who's in the kitchen. They don't know who the chef is, or if their food is being made by a man or a monkey. You'd have to advertise it well in advance, and the regulars would still be pissed if all their go-tos were not available. And if for any reason, Mr. Guest Chef screws up, then it's MY kitchen that gets the bad rap."

"Hmmm. Hadn't thought about that. Guess you're right."

"Of course I'm right. Now get the hell outta my kitchen with this guest chef shit." And he pointed a very large knife in my direction.

Back in the bar area, I pulled up my list and deleted "Guest chef." I'd ask him more about his Rock the Menu idea once he calmed down. He was ok that I'd be running front of house while Livia was gone, but believed the kitchen was his and his alone. I respected that. But bottom line, I was in charge.

Livia and I had sat down and done the schedule for while she was away. We also reviewed ordering food, liquor and paper goods, and all the linens, napkins, aprons, and bar towels. She signed a number of blank checks and put them in the safe for some of the smaller vendors whose accounts would need to be paid before she returned. While most of me felt comfortable with this, my stomach did a little flip when she dropped her keys in my hand. The restaurant was now mine.

Paris came in the next day just as we opened. "Hey, Boss Lady, looking good."

I told Wick to keep setting up the bar while I hopped into position and made my friend his Queen's Cosmo.

"So, now that you're in charge, I have some complaints." Paris tapped his black lacquered nails on the bar.

I studied his face to see if he was serious.

Laughing, he said, "Are you sure you're ready for this? I'm yanking your chain as always and will continue to do. You know me." He sipped his cocktail, closed his eyes, and purred.

"I don't care how high up the ladder you go; you are still in charge of my libations. Please. And thank you. Thank you very much." Paris was dressed in a red tuxedo suit with a black stripe down the pants and a black silk dress shirt with a red sequined skull bolo.

I studied the bolo and pulled up my idea for the logo on the phone. "What do you think of this for a logo for the bar? I'm thinking we need some merch. Mugs, bandanas and shirts. Maybe stickers." I watched the door as more customers trickled in.

"Not bad. Not bad. I got a hookup for advertising specialties if you need one. They can put that design on anything. Totes, water bottles... ooh a flask would be fun." Paris watched a tall, tan, well-dressed man with short curly brown hair slide by. He leaned off his stool in an exaggerated way to check out the man's behind. "I'll take a side of that, please."

The night ran smoothly. Only one customer had sent food back, saying her burger was overcooked. It wasn't, but we made her another one and removed the charge from her bill. She left happy.

Livia had done an excellent job creating a well-oiled machine, which of course, made my job easier. I was grateful she was so good at this, that we had such great staff, and a fabulous chef, and our regulars were wonderful people.

Niko came in not long before close and ordered the lemon chicken, a special on that night's menu. I'd watched earlier as Chef marinated the chicken in lemon juice, honey, garlic, salt, pepper, and tons of fresh basil. Then he'd sauteed it just prior to serving.

"This is so good, have you tasted it?" Niko closed his eyes and I could tell he was cataloging each ingredient in his mind. I loved watching this man eat.

"Yessss." I smiled.

"I know that look. What would you have done differently?" He pointed his fork in my direction.

I leaned across the bar and whispered, "Capers. I would have added capers during the sauté."

"Yes! Like chicken piccata. It would have been a lovely addition." He grabbed my hand, and kissed it several times over. "I love your palate. I simply love it."

I pulled my hand back. "Sir, if you will excuse me, I've got a restaurant to run." And with a wink I walked away.

46

∽

I mogene texted early on a Tuesday morning, saying she had news and would call me later that day. I could barely contain myself and called Paris.

"I think my genie might have some answers, but I'm worried about Henry. I haven't seen him since the D.D." I'd taken to referring to his black dot vanishing act as the Dot Disappearance.

"I hear you, girlfriend." Paris paused, "Let me put out this fire and call you right back. Better yet, I could use a croissant from the Station. Meet me there in thirty."

Always delighted to visit the wonderland of gourmet goodies and the glorious garden center, I hung up and jumped in the shower. *Oh, Henry, I hope this is it. I hope she's discovered everything you wanted to know.* Or did I? What if it 'completed' his sojourn here as a spirit and he could finally crossover? No longer a ghost. But maybe the black dots meant his departure anyway. I was both excited and scared to hear what Imogene had found.

*   *   *

"Hey there," I tried not to drool on the glass protecting those precious pastries: the chocolate croissants, the exquisite fruit tarts, and cinnamon swirls. "I'll have the pear galette and a large latte for here, thanks."

The place was packed for a Tuesday in winter, but the indoor dining area, which had a glass roof and glass walls, was warm and inviting. The scent of fresh baked sourdough bread, cookies and pastries pervaded the retail/ordering area, and I wondered if this was what heaven smelled like. Definitely *my* heaven.

I carried my sweet indulgence to a table overlooking the garden center filled with beautiful ceramic pots, fountains, and winter pansies. My latte arrived moments later. Taking a deep breath, I thought about Henry and where he was, or how he was. I just hoped he still 'was.'

A tall, stunning ebony man lowered himself elegantly into the chair on the other side of the table. His pants were a green shimmery material that reminded me of a mermaid.

"Hello, gorgeous. Any word from Casper?" Paris leaned back in the chair, oversized cat-eyed sunglasses wrapping his bald pate. He had on a white ruffled shirt with flared cuffs under a silver leather vest. It was fun watching people at surrounding tables scope him out without being too obvious.

"I'm scared. What if he's running out of time? I haven't found his family. I still don't know why he came to me, why I can see him—"

Paris held a hand up in front of my face. "Stop right there, sister. Why is this YOUR job? Why—" He put his hand to his chest. "Ohmigod. That's IT! Why *is* this your job? Because you're family! That's why you can see him when nobody else can. YOU'RE RELATED!" He slapped his hand on the table and the woman next to us jumped, then glared at him.

"Wait, what? No. Do you really believe that?" A warm feeling washed over me.

Just then my phone buzzed on the table next to my cup. A text from my genie. As I read it, I could feel the goosebumps rise on my arms.

I THINK YOU'RE RELATED TO HENRY.

I jumped up while shoving the phone in Paris' face, whispering *ohmigod ohmigod* while he read the text. His face lit with joy and he stood as well, and hugged me. "You're my new favorite psychic, Paris Savannah Harrison!" It was all I could do to keep from screaming.

Our conversation became so animated, we had to leave before we were thrown out. We continued in the parking lot, both of us so excited with the news. I couldn't wait to tell Henry. My phone rang. I answered and immediately put it on speaker. "Imogene! What's going on? What did you—how did you—" I paced around the parking lot until Paris steered me onto the grass.

She laughed. "This man is a relative! How fun is that? I was trying to remember how you came across his name in the first place—if you told me, I've forgotten."

My heart was about to leap out of my chest. Answers at last. This. Was. Amazing. I wanted to know exactly how we were related, but I could tell she wanted to share her journey of discovery. I held the phone between Paris and myself while I continued to hop from one foot to another.

"I felt bad that I wasn't having any luck with your request. It seemed very important to you, and I really hate to disappoint anyone, let alone someone whose father was such a gift to my family and countless others. You mentioned he'd already traced his lineage back several generations but you knew nothing about your mother's side. Whenever I hit a dead end with your mysterious gentlemen, I'd spend a little time on your mother's tree." With cars going by it was hard to hear, so I headed towards the garden area. Paris followed.

I began pacing again before Paris placed a hand on my shoulder and indicated I should stop. Then he signaled me to breathe. I gave him an exasperated look but sat on a stone bench holding the phone on my knee.

"Your mother's tree was the gift that kept on giving. Her entire line anchors close to Lewes, which is great. I'm familiar with the resources available here. Best of all, Henry's great, great granddaughter, Rose Dalton, kept a diary, and the Lewes Historical Society had a partial copy of it. Rose wrote a lot about her mother and grandmother's lives. They seemed particularly fond of your Mr. Talbot, who died rather tragically, I'm sad to say."

Rose. Rose Dalton. Henry's great, great granddaughter. My hand went to my heart. My poor Henry. I almost didn't want to know how he died.

"Do you want to set up a time to hear all this in person?"

I heard her teacup settle in its saucer. No way could I wait, although I'd want the whole story again, in person, for sure. "Can you give me some details now? I'm just so excited." The understatement of the year.

"Of course, dear. I totally understand. In the meantime, I'll send you your mother's family tree." She sipped her beverage and I heard the shuffle of papers. "I'll give you the Cliff notes version for now."

Paris tapped his watch that he had to run, mouthing 'I'm so sorry, call me later.' I nodded and decided to sit in my car, so I'd stop moving around. That way I could concentrate better and truly listen to her tale.

"Ok. Here we go. I traced your mother's line back to Sarah Hastings, your six times great grandmother. She married your Robert Henry Edward Talbot the second in seventeen ninety-six. They had a son that same year, Robert Henry Edward Talbot the third, and another son, Henry Edward George Talbot, four years later. My, they did love their English kings, did they not?" Imogene chuckled.

Well, Henry's mother did, I wanted to say, which made me smile. My life suddenly felt extraordinary. I had been conversing with my six times great grandfather—who gets to do that? Emotion welled inside of me.

"As I mentioned, your Mr. Talbot died in eighteen fifteen, I'm sorry to say, under very sad circumstances—"

"Can you tell me more about that later? I want to be able to take notes." I was lying. I wasn't ready to hear about his death. I first needed to hear about his life.

"Of course. Sarah married John Burton the year after Henry's death, and they had a daughter, Emily Jane."

It was a girl! Henry would have had a daughter for the very first time. I was so happy for him. And sad as well that he never got to meet her. My palms were sweating so I sat my phone on the dash with the speaker on.

"Are you ok?"

"Yes. Yes. Please go on." Vibrating with excitement, I put my hands on my legs to keep them from shaking.

"John Burton had been married before. His first wife died in childbirth. Very common in those days. He must have been delighted to have little Emily Jane."

Henry's Emily Jane, I thought.

"Then Emily married John Miller. So, she was Emily Jane Miller and guess what? She's buried in St. Peter's graveyard. How great is that?"

Wait, what? Emily Jane Miller... Emily Jane Miller. "Oh my god," I whisper.

"Indeed...—" Imogene continued on.

But I didn't hear what she was saying because that was the headstone where Henry kept reappearing. Emily Jane Miller. His daughter. I was laughing and crying now. No wonder I felt connected to him. Not only was he family, he was a father who couldn't leave his daughter, and I was a daughter who couldn't leave her father. I missed my dad terribly.

"Are you still there?"

"Yes. Sorry. I'm just excited that one of my relatives is buried in that cemetery. I love that." *Oh, Henry, where are you? I can't wait to share all this. Please be okay. Please be okay.*

Please be okay.

Please.

47

"I'm related to Henry! Ohmigod! I can't believe it never occurred to me; it seems so obvious." I practically screamed in run-on sentences to Niko while still in the parking lot at the Station.

"That," he stammered, "that is ... amazing."

I could tell Niko was not fully present. "What's going on? Is everything ok?"

"Yes, yes, of course. How are you related?"

There was still something in his voice. I wasn't sure I wanted to continue revealing all I'd learned till I knew better what was going on. "Um, are you free later? We could meet for a drink, and I can tell you everything live and in person."

"Yes. That would be best."

He was surprisingly formal. What the hell? We made plans to meet at Irish Eyes. I wanted to sit somewhere where I could look out over the water.

I sat in my car in a state of wonder. The parking lot was nearly empty and the temperature outside had dropped significantly. I was too excited about the news to spend time worrying about what was going on with Niko. Being Henry's six times great granddaughter made me giddy. I had such a tremendous fondness for this man. His energy, his demeanor—all of which reminded me so much of my dad. Then I remembered the black spots and my joy was somewhat dampened. What did it mean? We were just getting started, I couldn't lose him now. I needed to find him.

I checked the bench near the caboose, then the Zwaanendael Museum, the cemetery, and the beach. No sign anywhere. Damn. An hour later, sitting in my car, looking at the Bay, I was running such a mix of emotions: excitement and joy to share my news, fear and angst that I might lose him, and an uneasy feeling about Niko.

Niko.

I loved him. Wow. I really did. My heart was wide open with the news about Henry, and I could finally shove aside my fears and admit this to myself. The knowledge warmed me to my core. Niko and I were great together. I couldn't wait to see him to share my feelings and the news.

He'd beaten me to Irish Eyes but knew the seats that I loved in the bar area next to the window, overlooking the water. Most of the slips were empty, but one or two boats remained. I watched him sip a Jameson on the rocks, which was what he drank when he was more contemplative. When he was high energy and on the move, it was a Pinot. I loved that I knew this about him. I also knew that when he tasted a dish and felt the balance was perfect, his forehead was smooth and relaxed. When he felt the dish needed something, a little line appeared between his brows.

"I wasn't sure what you were in the mood for." His eyes were dark. His body tense.

"This." I threw my arms around him and kissed him passionately, not caring that we were in a public space. Then I hugged him till I felt his body relax. I held on to his shoulders, and looked deep into his eyes. "I love you. I...love everything about you. You are just the most incredible man and I love being with you."

Niko shook his head slowly and looked like he was going to cry.

I exhaled like I'd been holding my breath for years, and in many ways, I had. Saying all this out loud was so freeing. Like I could have levitated right off the ground. While so much was riding on what he said next, I was still proud that I had acknowledged those feelings and said everything I wanted to say.

"I... I love you too." He ran his thumb along my jawline. Then he gathered me into his arms, held me tight and whispered in my ear, "You are the song my heart sings."

We stayed that way for a while. I let my body melt into his, relishing the strength of him, the cedarwood smell of him, the wonder of him.

When we finally let go, I sat back on my stool, grinning. Niko sighed and turned his gaze to the water.

"What is it?" I felt as though a huge dark cloud had just overshadowed the sun.

He swirled the amber liquid around his glass. "Gramercy on the Green has offered me sous-chef."

"Holy shit." Amazing. He'd be second in command. We'd talked about Gramercy last week as they'd just received their first Michelin star. It was on his top ten list but Gramercy was also in New York.

He set his glass down and ran his hands through his gorgeous hair. "I honestly don't know what to do." Grabbing my right hand, he kissed my palm and held it to his cheek. "And knowing you love me makes this even harder."

Not knowing what to say or think, I sat dumbfounded. I got the news about Henry just as I thought he might disappear. I poured my heart out to Niko, and he had an offer in New York. Part of me wanted to laugh at the ridiculousness of it all, and part of me wanted to cry.

"It comes down to how important it is for me to be known in this field, or how much I want to run my own show. And then ..." Niko paused and looked almost distraught. "Then there's you. Until today, I would not have asked you to come to New York. I wasn't sure exactly what we had, or what we were doing, though I knew I loved being with you. But I also knew you had me at arm's length, and how could you not? That jerk left you at the altar. Who's to say you would ever trust any man ever again?"

"Thank you. Thank you for saying that." He saw me and he truly loved me. I gave his shoulder a little squeeze. "So, your choices are, one: being the star of the kitchen in your own small-town restaurant, or two: getting next to top billing in a Michelin star New York restaurant. Niko—those are amazing choices. Like, seriously. It's not as if you were choosing between the army and working on your uncle's farm. This is fabulous. *And* a testament to your culinary genius. I'm happy for you."

And I was. Whatever the future brought, we'd deal with it. Where we sat overlooked the canal, and I swear the sun dazzled the water even more.

48

Despite all that we'd shared, Niko still wanted to hear about Henry.

"Well, we're related. Don't you love it? I'm his six times great granddaughter. I'm sure it's why I can see him. At least, that's what I think. And his wife had a baby girl. But not before she married another man. But then the daughter grew up and got married and is buried in the very spot he returns to most in the cemetery." I stopped to breathe, realizing I'd said all that in a rush.

"That's amazing." Niko sat up straight, crossing his arms. "This is on your mother's side of the family?" His eyes shone.

"Yes! I'd never traced that side. And there are relatives on that side that my mother has never mentioned and may not even know. I haven't had a chance to call her since I spoke with Imogene."

We sipped in silence for a moment, when Niko's phone buzzed.

"Oh, crap. I need to go. I'm meeting a contractor to go over my ideas for the layout of the restaurant. Do you want to come?" He stood, pulling out his wallet.

I shook my head. "I'm going to see if I can get a hold of my mom. You go."

He kissed the top of my head and left.

Back home I settled on my loveseat, coffee in hand. What a day. *What* a day. I dialed my mom, eager to share the news. Even though I rarely called, my mom didn't pick up. She wasn't a fan of texting either, but I sent the note, 'Big news' anyway, hoping for a response. While I waited, I hopped on my computer to open the family tree that Imogene had sent over. Holy shit, there was Henry. I squealed with delight, jumped up and did a little dance. Seeing it made me so happy. I raised my glass of wine. "Here's to family."

Minutes later, my phone rang.

"Genna," my mother said, in that husky, Demi Moore voice of hers, "is everything ok? Well, you said it was big news, so of course it is. Did you meet someone? Are you going back to school?"

I felt as though the wind had left my sails. I was used to her inquiries about my love life, but school? Is that what big news meant to her?

"Genevieve. Are you still there?"

All of a sudden, the news felt different to me, and I wasn't sure how much I wanted to reveal, "Yeah, Mom. I've learned some things about your genealogy, and I thought I'd share."

"Oh." Her voice went completely flat. "I guess I never had that much interest in it."

I wasn't sure how to respond. "I was excited to learn that a relative of ours is buried in St. Peters." *And that I'm related to someone who happens to be a ghost, but let's hold on that for now.*

"Oh. Who is that?"

"Her name is Emily Jane Miller and she's our, well, she's my five times great grandmother. Imogene traced your line back through your mother to the late seventeen hundreds." I didn't understand her apathy. I thought she'd be more excited.

"Huh."

I sipped my coffee, but it had grown cold. My mother never said 'huh'. Weird. Wasn't sure what to say, or how hard to press. "Should I call you later? Sounds like a bad time."

"No, no. I'm sorry." She sighed. "Genealogy was always Daddy's thing. And we happened to go sailing today with some friends, and I really missed him." Now I got it. I could hear the grief in her voice. It made me tremendously sad, but pleased that she had shared it with me.

"Oh, Mom. I miss him every day." We rarely talked about him.

"Tell me again who's buried in St. Pete's?" I heard the chink of ice in a glass.

Part of me wished we could continue talking about my father, just for a minute, but I knew better. So, I repeated as much as I remembered Imogene saying and promised to forward a copy of her family tree.

"Well, if you really are interested in my history, I have a couple of things passed down through the women in our family. I seem to remember a diary, a few photographs, and a tiny painting. In fact, I think the photographs and the painting are still in a plastic bin in the garage. I'm pretty sure of it." It sounded like my mother was pacing as we spoke. "It's about the size of a shoe box with a blue lid."

Oh. My. God. A diary? Was that the diary Imogene had spoken of? And the photos and painting were in the space beneath my feet. Mom promised to look for the diary, and we said our goodbyes. I quickly put my shoes back on and headed down the stairs, excited for the search.

The garage smelled of gasoline, dirt and mildew. It was also really cold and I wished I'd thought to grab my jacket. There were at least twenty boxes wedged into gray metal shelving and I had no idea where to start. Plus, there was just one overhead bulb, and despite the afternoon light, it was dark inside. I ran back upstairs, grabbed a jacket and my keys and backed my Jeep out so I'd have more room. I also left the door up despite the cold, so I could see what the hell I was doing.

The first box contained my high school yearbooks, so I quickly moved on to the next. And the next. And the one after that. About a dozen boxes later, I came across a box with some fabric, carefully wrapped in layers of plastic, and underneath, a small plastic box with photos in it. Setting that one carefully on the workbench, I shoved the rest back on the shelves and closed the garage door. I'd pull my car in later. I was too excited to get back upstairs.

My phone had been buzzing like crazy, so I checked to make sure all was well at the pub. It was Paris wanting more details, so we agreed to meet for a late dinner at Cultured Pearl, a sushi restaurant in Rehoboth.

Sitting at my little table, I carefully removed the lid and was delighted to see dozens of black and white photos. Some from the forties and fifties, some older. No one I recognized. Gently setting those aside, I found an old handkerchief with yellowed lace, a rosary with black beads, and a small leather booklet. It was about two inches by three inches and had a little clasp on the side.

My phone buzzed again but I ignored it.

Framed by an oval was a hand painted portrait of a woman in a cornflower blue dress with blonde ringlets. But what made me gasp were the unmistakable, icy blue eyes of Henry Talbot staring back at me. Emily Jane. I couldn't wait to show Henry his daughter.

49

Breakfast at the Station, drinks with Niko at Irish Eyes, now a late dinner with Paris at the Pearl. I never got tired of eating out—always something new to learn—always something new to explore. We sat at a two-top looking out at Rehoboth Avenue through floor to ceiling windows. The restaurant was located on the second and third floor of a building in downtown Rehoboth. Inside, there was bamboo everywhere, along with Asian artwork and decorated cloth panels. In the summer, the popular spot was their rooftop deck, with tables surrounded by koi ponds. From our perch we had primo seats to watch people stroll by on the sidewalk below.

"You never called me back. After I left you in the parking lot at the Station, you were supposed to give me the deets on Imogene's findings." Paris chided me. He wore a white linen shirt underneath a blue brocade jacket.

"Oh, my friend. We have much to discuss. Let's start with, I told Niko I loved him, and guess what? That crazy Greek loves me right back." I laughed. Happier than I could remember for a long time, I'd dressed up. A black sweater mini dress, tights, and black knee-high boots with a three-inch heel which put me at just over six feet. I was ready to be seen.

Paris stood and applauded, then gracefully sat back down. "I LOVE this. I'm so happy for you. It's about time. When did— what did—how did I miss this?" He reached across the table and squeezed my hand.

"Niko also got an offer from a Michelin starred restaurant in New York." I paused, letting *that* sink in.

"Stop, stop, stop! Good grief. Start from when I saw you and tell me EVERYTHING." Paris demanded.

Our server cruised by to check on drinks. Paris held his empty martini glass up with both hands saying, "More, please."

It was so great to be able to share all this with him. How I was finally able to push aside my fears and admit that I loved Niko. And how wonderful it was that he loved me right back. That, as Niko put it so beautifully, I was the song his heart sang. Paris loved that.

As I reiterated my remarkable day to my fabulous friend, I expanded on everything I'd been thinking about. I owned every bit of it, falling in love, the restaurant industry, and really, for the first time, fully embracing who I was. Like how I loved cookbooks. That I read them like novels, diving into the introduction, imagining the cook behind the recipes, eager to learn whether they were embracing long held culinary traditions passed down through their family or trying for something new and outside the box. Each and every one was a delightful introduction to yet another food lover like myself. I accepted and was fine with the fact that cooking did not bring me the same joy it did Niko or Cleveland. I had no desire to preside over a kitchen staff, slicing, dicing, steaming, and sautéing, night after night, tucked away in the back, cooking for dozens of people. Though tasting and rethinking recipes was great fun, I wanted front of house, I wanted to be seen, and I wanted a stake in the game. And somehow, though I couldn't fully explain, Henry was a part of this. He had seen me.

I also wanted to be part of something that held an element of fun. An experience. To create a space where everyone felt welcome, felt a sense of community and a sense of joy when they walked through the door.

Starving, we ordered the Mexican edamame with jalapeno and cilantro, the pork gyoza, the Zorro roll with shrimp and chiles, the Red Dragon roll with spicy tuna and avocado, and the Korean fried cauliflower. As I sipped my second Kappa Tini, a delightful libation made with cucumber vodka, simple syrup and lime, I was more than ready to talk about Henry. With Niko, everything that had transpired filled me with such joy that I was even okay entertaining that he might go to New York. Not my first choice, for sure, but he wasn't leaving me at the altar. With or without him, I'd set my path, grateful to have found my footing.

But Henry was different. All the excitement of getting answers, finding we were related, just the sheer experience of meeting this wonderful spirit was overshadowed by how he was changing. What it all meant. I feared I was losing him.

"I am Henry's six times great granddaughter."

"Of course you are. How did I not see this before?" Paris expertly grabbed a roll with his chopsticks.

"And the stone in the cemetery where he always returns to is..." I did a drum roll on the table. "His daughter's!"

"What? Are you serious right now?" Paris put down his chopsticks and sat back in his chair. "This is amazing."

"I know, right? His wife married a man named John Burton, so Henry's daughter became Emily Jane Burton. But then, she married a man named John Miller. So that's why the tombstone says Emily Jane Miller. And..." I handed him the portrait from my purse. "It's her, Paris."

Paris' eyes filled with tears as he reached for the picture.

"I knew the minute I saw it who she was. I know you've never seen him, but Henry has these amazing icy blue eyes. And hers are just like his."

A large table of older women in the middle of the restaurant began singing happy birthday. I grinned. There was a lot to celebrate.

50

Knowing Henry was related was such a gift. I couldn't wait to share the news about his family, his daughter's life, where she was buried, and me.

Every day before work, I made the circuit looking for Henry: caboose, beach, Shipcarpenter campus, cemetery. If I wasn't working, I did it twice. At the pub I'd watch the cemetery till the sun went down.

Weeks went by. I couldn't believe after all this time, when I finally had answers, Henry was gone. *He can't be. He just can't.*

Livia had returned from her excursion looking tan and more relaxed than ever, which made her look even younger. There was definitely a bounce in her step that hadn't been there before.

"Welcome back." I grinned, giving her a big hug.

"Well, look at you. Running a restaurant. Cleveland said you were great. Come sit, I want to hear all about it." She led the way to a table near the window. Her tee shirt was lime green with white lettering that said, 'In my defense, I was left unsupervised.' She smelled like coconut.

I studied her as we sat. The light was already coming in through the stained glass, which left triangles of color reflecting on some of the tables. "You look great. Whatever this did for you, it definitely worked."

Patting my hand, Livia said, "I feel good. I so needed that. Not just a break, but to take a breath. I think sometimes I feel like if I'm not here twenty-four seven, it all goes away. And doing it on my own, day after day, is exhausting. Not that I don't have the best staff, 'cause I do." She paused around the room. "This is such a part of who I am. But this trip showed me balance."

I was so pleased for her.

Livia's face got a funny expression that I couldn't exactly read. Then she went to the bar, pulled out a Macallan, her favorite scotch, and brought back two rocks glasses. "Join me?" she asked.

I indicated a tiny amount by pinching my thumb and finger together.

She looked around the room, studying the space as though she'd never seen it before. The brick wall closest to the cemetery held wooden replicas of tavern signs. The opposite wall was forest green and featured tasteful watercolors of Ireland and also a ship and some pirates painted by the famous Howard Pyle. Each wall was framed by dark stained mahogany pillars that matched the bar. "Vie. This is home. I've built a community here. This is my family." She paused. "I am, though, bringing George on as an investment partner. He's got the most amazing business head on his shoulders and lets me discuss my beloved Grace ad nauseum. His funds will allow us to upgrade the kitchen, particularly the ovens and the dishwasher." She sipped her amber goodness slowly, raising the glass up to the light now pouring in through the front window. "I can't tell you how wonderful it feels to have someone to share this with, who happens to be my lover as well." She winked, then sipped again.

"George is great. I'm glad he makes you happy."

I had wondered, briefly, if Livia would come home and tell us she was retiring, so I was pleased to know that Grace O'Malley's would stay the same and that Livia would still be here.

When I had played out the Livia retirement scenario in my head, it included the possibility of me buying Grace, or buying into it. But as we sat here, I realized I could never really make it my own. It was hers, through and through. And although I loved Niko, and Niko made *me* happy, if he moved to New York, he'd most likely be going alone. I'd be heartbroken, but Lewes was *my* home. Always had been, always would be. Whatever I built would have to be here.

As if reading my mind, Livia said, "And how are things with that handsome Greek of yours?"

"Funny you should ask." I said, tapping my lips. "I told him that I loved him, and he said it right back, which was awesome."

"Ain't love grand?" Livia raised her glass. "Sláinte," she said, which was Irish for 'cheers'. "I also heard he was possibly going to open a restaurant here." She cocked her head.

Of course, she would know. This woman was tuned in even when she was on the other side of the world.

"Possibly." I took a deep breath. "He also has a sous chef offer in New York at one of his top ten favorite restaurants. So, we'll see." I shrugged then sipped. "Let's hope he stays. Why is life so complicated?" Our glasses were empty. I picked up the bottle and held it over her glass with a question on my face.

"No, I'm good, luv. There's another way to look at this you know." She took the bottle from my hand and set it down. Then cupped my chin in her hand and said, "Don't think of them as complications; think of them as possibilities. I never expected a George to walk into my life, but when you do find someone who's got your back, loves you for you, and believes in your dreams, well, there's nothing like it." And she hugged me.

Living by the water fed my soul. My home was here. My found family was here. But life without Niko would be empty.

"He hasn't asked me to go." I picked up the bottle and the glasses to put them away.

Livia put a hand out, stopping me. "If New York is what he chooses, he will ask," she said. "And when he does, don't let fear make the decision for you."

51

*n*iko texted me early the next morning. *Are you awake? Can we talk? Better yet, can I come make breakfast for you?*

Well, hell yeah to that, I thought, still in bed. I texted back *Sure. You know where the key is.*

A minute later I heard him sprint up the stairs, taking them two at a time. I sat up, realizing he must have been parked outside the house. It made me giggle.

He practically flew to the bed, scooped me into his arms, kissed me like a madman, then slower, pressing his lips gently to my eyelids, my cheeks, my nose, my neck. I could feel my body melting beneath him.

We made love without another word, which left me breathless. He loved me. He really loved me. I let the warmth of that wash over me and over me again. Then we lay together side by side under the skylight, staring up at a new day. Breaking the silence, he turned, propping himself up on one arm.

"I really love you, you know. I've loved you from the first moment we talked about food, and I saw your passion for it. Every time something happens, I want to share it with you. You. Just you."

The way he said this, the way he looked at me, I mean, wow. I'd never felt this way with Logan, or anyone for that matter. It was wonderful and amazing and delicious all at once. I'd embraced my fear. Made room for it. Turning to him, I said, "I love you too. It's scary as hell, but I do." I studied his beautiful face, seeing that hint of amber in those dark eyes. Tracing his jawline, I felt happier than I had in a very long time. "Does that mean you're still gonna make me breakfast?" *And stay in Lewes*, I wanted to add, but thought better of it.

He leaned forward till his head touched mine. "Your wish is my command."

* * *

We sat on the floor with our backs to the couch, the little wagon coffee table now hosting an assortment of fruit, cheeses, and a beautiful omelet. Some of this must have come up the stairs with him, 'cause my fridge wasn't this well stocked. I could hear birds singing outside with the promise of a new day.

Desperate to get out of my head where scaredy cat Vie and in-love Vie were arguing, I asked, "Are you opening a restaurant in Lewes or are you going to ask me to move to New York?" There. I'd said it.

He paused with a bite of omelet halfway to his mouth. Setting the fork down, he looked thoughtful. "As much as Gramercy would be a huge feather in my cap, and open doors for me everywhere, I really want my own place, you know? I don't want to share the kitchen. What do you think? Am I crazy?"

"Yesssssssss! I mean, no, you're not crazy, but YES, you're going to open a restaurant! Yes, yes, yes!" I threw my arms around him. "Are you sure? This is really what you want?" Relief flooded me. I wouldn't lose him to the Big Apple, fame, and fortune.

"It's really what I want. And you. I. Want. You."

52

∾

Paris and I had agreed to meet for lunch at Saketumi, an Asian restaurant between Rehoboth and Lewes. He was sitting at the bar when I arrived, sipping a green concoction.

"Cucumber margarita martini?" I pointed to the glass.

"You know it." He tipped it in my direction.

Mike, a fellow bartender extraordinaire, was behind the bar. "Hey, Vie." He pointed to Paris' drink. "Same?"

"Not just yet. Jasmine tea, thanks."

My friend Emily, who worked there as well, stopped over to say hi. "I got it, Mike." Giving me a quick squeeze, she said she'd be right back with my tea.

"No drinkie poo for you? What's that about?" Paris was dressed in a navy-blue suit with white polka dots, navy silk t-shirt, white pocket handkerchief, and sequined loafers. He smelled like tobacco and vanilla.

"I'm working after this and when I start drinking at noon I just wanna go home and take a nap. What are you wearing? Not your usual scent."

"Tom Ford." Paris studied me carefully. "You look like a woman who's been fluffed, folded, and loved. Tell me everything."

I threw my head back and laughed loudly. "This is all your fault, you know. All. Your. Fault." I glanced at the menu but was thinking about how lovely it was being in bed with Niko. Talking food with Niko. Talking life with Niko. Oh, God, was I in love. It felt so wonderful, I almost felt guilty. Like a part of me didn't deserve this happiness. Your found family. And Henry, who was now real family, which was amazing. And then, Niko. My Niko.

"Niko got a job offer in New York." I threw that out, just to get a reaction.

Paris pointed his chopsticks at me. "Oh, no, you don't. You are not leaving me for the Big Apple."

Emily sat a huge tray of sushi between us. There was the usual Crunchy Spicy Tuna, Philadelphia Spring Roll, and one gorgeous roll I didn't recognize. We hadn't ordered, but they knew what we liked.

"What's that?" I asked, pointing at the new arrival.

"Chef's choice. He saw Paris come in." Emily smiled.

Paris made a face that said he knew he was the shit, and I cracked up once again. Everyone found my friend irresistible. The high tops in the bar area were now full, and the din had increased. Other servers who knew us gave a little wave as they cruised in and out between the tables.

"You know, Stewart, I haven't seen you laugh like this since before Mr. A-Hole left your lovely self on the beach. I like it. It suits." Paris wielded his chopsticks over the chef's choice and popped one in his mouth. "Oh, my goodness. This is amazing. Mmm. Mmm." Sipping his martini, he once again jabbed his chopsticks at me, clacking them with each word. "You. Are. Not. Moving."

"No, I'm not. He'll open a restaurant here. We're staying."

"Oh, WE are, are we?" Paris dabbed his forehead with the black cloth napkin that had been laying in his lap. "Well, thank goodness. A good bartender is hard to find."

I poked him with my sticks, which I had yet to use.

"I knew that boy was talented. Glad we can keep him." Paris said. "Who's his backers?"

The bar itself was now full, but Mike kept an eye on us. Alec, another fabulous bartender, was shaking the metal cocktail shaker. I loved that sound. Mike pointed a finger at me. I looked at Paris' nearly empty glass and indicated two more, meaning one for me, as well.

"Two of the investors are Bill and Jake from Five Points Ventures..."

Before I could finish, Paris interjected, "Oh, great choices! Niko did well."

Paris knew the good, the bad, and the ugly about everyone. People loved sharing the latest dirt with him, because his reactions were always exaggerated. Fortunately, he himself rarely gossiped and I loved that. Despite the hundreds of thousands of tourists who came through our little swath of paradise, the year-round populations of our beach towns were small. Words, especially the unkind ones, spread like fire.

"Well, I'm very happy for Niko. But more importantly, I'm very happy for you." Paris swiveled on his bar stool, so he faced me. "You deserve all good things. Oh, before I forget, how's your ghostie? You haven't mentioned him, so now I know you're in love."

"Oh, Paris. I haven't seen him. I'm so worried." I frowned. "He still doesn't know we're related." I inhaled deeply. I felt such sadness about Henry. While I couldn't wait to share the news of our ancestry, I worried even his spirit time was coming to an end.

53

My meeting with Imogene had come at last. We met in one of the meeting rooms at the new Lewes library, and when I got there the first thing I noticed was the family tree on a large piece of paper, front and center.

"Oh, Imogene, I can't thank you enough." I stood beside the table so I could see the whole tree. This was one of the smaller rooms with just one table and four chairs, and we had it all to ourselves.

"C'mon, girl. Sit. Sit." She gazed up at me through large, green glasses with square frames. Her hair was once again in a bun, with chopsticks through it rather than pencils, and she wore a bright, multi-colored sweater. "Oh my," she said, looking me over. "You look just like your dad."

Smiling, I tucked a stray hair behind one ear. "Yeah, I do." It'd been said before, but I was always happy to hear it.

"I'm so glad I started noodling your mother's family tree. I wanted to be able to give you *something*, and I felt bad that I wasn't having any luck with your Henry. Then lo and behold, there he was. It was a lovely surprise."

I couldn't take my eyes off the chart that sat before me with Henry and Sarah at the top, then daughter, after daughter, after daughter, down to me. "This is just so cool."

"What was really helpful was the diary. The Lewes Historical Society doesn't have the original, or an entire copy, but what they have was fun to read. I brought a copy for you to take with." She pushed a small stack of xeroxed papers toward me, revealing the handwriting of more than one author, some messy ink blobs, and a few with tears. "They talk a lot about your Henry and what a lovely man he was. Unfortunately, as I mentioned he died tragically. It was just after the War of Eighteen Twelve."

I knew The War of 1812, which lasted almost three years, had come to Lewes in the Spring of 1813. The British demanded that the city provide them with fresh provisions, or they would destroy the town. Lewes said no. The British waited three weeks for us to change our mind, but we didn't. Pissed off, they began firing on the town on April Sixth. We fought back and the British withdrew twenty-two hours later. No one in Lewes was killed, so I knew that wasn't how Henry had died.

"As you know, the British fired on us for almost twenty-four hours during April eighteen thirteen." Imogene pulled her glasses off and began to clean them. "I believe over eight hundred projectiles were fired upon the town, including the first use of the Congreve rocket."

"Is that right?" I was trying to be polite, but having Livia as my boss as well as a father who loved this shit, I knew it well.

"You know cannonballs don't explode, right? They cause damage by their weight and velocity."

Nodding, I said nothing, hoping we could get past the history lesson. One wall of the room was all glass, and I watched a group of kids go by laughing and talking on their way to story hour.

Imogene continued, "I'm assuming the cannonballs that were found were collected and returned to the proper authorities, as they could be reused against the enemy. I would also imagine young boys around town competed with each other to find as many as they could. Some of these were in the water, and there's notes in the diary about a teenage boy who was determined to retrieve one, even during a storm. Henry and his oldest son, Robert Henry Edward Talbot the third, were near the water that afternoon, saw the boy go in, but not come out. Henry the third went in after the boy, but it was your Henry that ended up rescuing them both. His body washed ashore the following day and he was buried at his farm."

Oh, Henry. My heart ached knowing all he'd missed.

Cannonball House

54

∽

"I think we should go with Olive. It's simple, yet elegant."
Niko said. He and I were wrapped around each other in
bed, discussing the restaurant.

"We should." I said, delighting in the 'we.'

Suddenly he sat up, looking very serious. "I want to ask you
something and I want you to take all the time you need to think
about it. There's no wrong answers. Got it?"

Oh, dear God. Now what. He wasn't going to propose. No.
No. No. What could it be? I sat up as well, feeling my face get
warm. "What...what is it?" I stammered.

He reached for my hand. "I want you to manage Olive. Run
front of house. You'd be perfect and I would love to do this
with you. I can't think of anyone more qualified, or frankly," he
kissed my hand, "more fun."

I sagged with relief, then threw myself at him. "Yes, YES! Of
course I will. I'd love to. Are you serious right now? Ohmigod,
YES!"

He pushed me out to arm's length. "Are you sure? What
about Grace O'Malley's?"

I knew Livia would understand. Especially with the Walrus by her side.

We sat at my little table and beamed at each other over coffee and yogurt with fresh berries. I was so happy I almost vibrated right off the chair.

"Thank you," Niko said. "You've just made me the happiest chef in the world."

"Excellent." I raised my cup. "Here's to Olive. Our restaurant." We chinked.

"Slight delay, though." His brow creased. "My third backer is moving to Florida. His dad has taken ill, and he's going to go spend time there. It's all good. I have a few other interested parties."

I heard car doors slam in the driveway. No doubt my renters were taking their kids to school.

"Well, I have a question for you." I took a deep breath. "I'm thrilled you want me to manage. I know it's going to be a lot of hard work and we're in this new relationship, but I totally believe in this, and us. I believe in us." I paused, gathering courage, then got up and started pacing.

"What is it?" He reached for me and pulled me into his lap. "Tell me." His eyes searched my face.

"If I'm going to be a part of it, then I'd like to invest in Olive." I bit my lower lip. "My dad set aside monies for med school. A trust fund, for my future. And this is it. This is the future I want." God, it felt good to say that.

Niko's eyes shone as he took my face in his hands and kissed me. "Then we're doing this. We're really doing this."

55

∽

I couldn't wait to tell Livia the news.

"Whaaaat? Genevieve Stewart. That. Is. Amazing." She clapped her hands in delight.

"You're not upset?" I reached over and rested a hand on her knee.

"How could I not wish this for you? This is what you were born to do. The idea of you and Niko sharing this new endeavor warms my heart."

She'd been wonderfully supportive, knowing she'd still have me for another six to eight months while we gutted the rowhouse and made it our own. Fortunately, it had been zoned commercial for some time, having been a boutique prior to our acquisition.

Paris was equally pleased and happy not to lose his favorite bartender.

No matter how much Niko and I talked about it, I never tired of going over every little detail about our venture. This is what happens when you choose something you love. Surprisingly, we argued over very little. Niko was all about the food, Mediterranean with a twist, lots of small plates…tapas style dishes. I was all about everything else: the look of the menus, what servers would wear, the color of the tablecloths. The only thing we really debated was plates and bowls. Niko wanted white porcelain; I leaned towards the more trendy stoneware.

On my days off, we slept at Niko's. The nights I worked, we slept at mine.

When I woke that morning, there were drops of rain on the skylight. I didn't even own an umbrella, preferring to pull up the hood on my raincoat.

Later the rain stopped. I'd left early for work and found myself standing in front of the former home of Gilbert McCracken, built in 1765. It had been a restaurant, a laundry store, even the mayor's office. But now it belonged to the Lewes Historical Society and was known as the Cannonball House, as there was one lodged in its foundation.

Cannonball. As I stared at the one in front of me, I kept going over Imogene's story trying to understand how Henry's tragedy had occurred in the first place. They couldn't possibly have seen a cannonball through the waves, especially in a storm. It must have been a spot where others had been found. But why was Henry there? How was Henry there? It was as if I could poke enough holes in the story, then it wouldn't have happened. Shouldn't have happened. Then Henry would have met his lovely daughter, Emily Jane.

I carried the miniature with me everywhere I went. She was the spitting image of her father, with her icy blue eyes and sweet smile. The artist had put her in a satiny blue dress, making her eyes even more beautiful. Her hair was blonde and styled in the ringlets of the era. From the research Imogene had done, I believed the painting was on a piece of porcelain.

The parts of the diary I'd received from Imogene referred to Henry as someone who was kind, dependable, and intensely curious. How his wife Sarah had mourned his loss, but happily delivered a healthy baby girl. Then eventually remarried a man who had lost a wife and son in childbirth years earlier. A silver lining in a very sad tale.

I'd walked from my carriage apartment, taking a slight detour on my way to Grace. The Cannonball house was east of there, on First Street. From the Cannonball house, I wandered to the cemetery at St. Peter's, to visit the grave of Emily Jane.

"Miss Vie."

"Henry!" It was all I could do not to throw my arms around him. He looked fairly solid at this point, but something was different. I couldn't quite put my finger on it.

"Henry." I pointed at the tombstone. "This is your daughter. Emily Jane is your daughter!"

"My daughter? How is this possible?" There was a shimmer to him I hadn't seen before. Oh, shit, Henry. What was happening? My heart beat faster.

"Your wife had a baby girl and named her Emily Jane, and the following year married your neighbor, John Burton. Then Emily grew up and married John Miller which is why the stone says Emily Jane Miller." All of this came out in a rush. I was so excited I could barely breathe. Hopefully he'd liked Burton. The diary said he was a good and decent man.

"She married John Burton." Henry crossed his arms and nodded. "Well, well. I liked John." He stepped closer to the headstone and laid a hand gently on it. "My daughter." He turned towards me again. "I have a daughter. This is a great day indeed."

"And there's a diary. Emily's great granddaughter, Rose, kept a journal of the stories handed down through the women in your family."

"Is that so? Rose. Well, I'll be." Henry glowed as he touched the headstone. "And I have a daughter. Emily Jane."

Then I remembered the miniature. "Oh! I have a portrait of her. According to the diary, it was a gift from her husband, John, on their wedding day. She looks just like you."

I held the tiny picture close, and his face lit up like a lantern. He covered his mouth with one hand as his shoulders shook with emotion. Then he turned away from me, wiping his eyes, though I could see no tears. "Oh, my sweet Vie. How can I ever thank you?"

"Well," I continued. "That's what family does. I'm your six times great granddaughter." My voice shook as I said it. I barely got the words out, I was so emotional. The skies darkened and I feared the rain would return.

Henry's eyes got very round as he stared at me, then he whooped. "My Genevieve! Oh, my Genevieve!" His joy was palpable. He folded his arms around himself and kept shaking his head. Reaching a hand towards my face, no hesitation this time, he cupped the side of it. Though it felt a bit like a cold, wet washcloth, I didn't flinch. Just smiled.

There was a now a definite shimmer to his whole body and my heart slammed against my chest. No, I thought. *Henry, no. Please.* We just found each other. I'd seen so many movies where the ghost leaves at the end. Noooo. This couldn't be. Not now. Not ever, if I had my way. *I can't lose you too, Henry.*

"Forgive me, Genevieve." My name slowly rolled off his tongue. "I don't believe I've thanked you enough. This is absolutely the greatest gift. You can't know what it means to me, but the fact that you are family as well ..." His voiced wavered, "Is more than I could ask for."

There was so much I wanted to say, but I was too choked up to respond, so I nodded.

"I've been having dreams of Sarah, my wife. Or maybe they aren't dreams at all, because I heard her say clearly as you were revealing my daughter, 'Oh for pity's sake, Henry, it's about time.'" He chuckled. "'Took you long enough', she said."

Emotionally I was being doused alternately by relief, then fear. Joy, then pain. Relief that I'd been able to discover what had happened to his family. Given him the answers he'd sought for so many years. Fear that this meant his departure to another plane. That he'd no longer be visible to me. Available to me. Joy at watching him embrace his daughter, knowing things had turned out all right, despite his untimely death. Pain at the thought of losing Henry. My Henry. I wanted to hug him, comfort him, but I knew my arms would just pass through. So, I stood as close to him as I could without touching and together we gazed upon the tombstone of his daughter, who I now knew was my relative too.

A few people had been wandering around the cemetery. They couldn't see Henry, but I was emotional, and folks tended to avoid that.

"Emily had a daughter whom she named Henrietta. After you." I smiled, so pleased to deliver this news.

"What?" Henry put his hand on his heart. "How delightful!" Then he looked puzzled. "How did you know?"

"There's a diary..." I paused as Henry turned his head like something had distracted him.

"Oh, you did say that, and I got caught up in the moment. My apologies. Tell me more. That is, if you have time." Henry glanced towards the bar.

"Yes! Your wife Sarah outlived John Burton by ten years, but then went to live with her daughter—your daughter—and her family until she passed in eighteen thirty-six. Sarah's buried somewhere on your homestead—near a tree with twin trunks?"

Henry's eyes closed. "It was her favorite spot. We often sat there and discussed our boys, our lives, our future." His body was more transparent than it had been moments ago. "Miss Vie, um, Genevieve, my wife... I believe she's calling me, I think." He paused, his face a mixture of wonder and joy.

"Oh, Henry." *Please don't leave*, I wanted to say, but how long had he been here? How long had he waited to be with his family once again, for I believed that's what was happening.

Had he sensed it too? "You'll be all right, sweet child. I know you will." He gave me such a look of love, a sob escaped me. Then suddenly, he was gone.

I sank to my knees in front of Emily's grave and let the tears flow. I knew I wouldn't see him again, and it broke my heart. Had we said everything we needed to say? Maybe. I hadn't told him how he died, but did it matter? Sarah had called him home.

Without a sound, I was enveloped in long arms that I could immediately tell belonged to my sweet Niko. "I'm here, my love."

"Henry's gone. Really gone." I leaned back into my rock.

"I gathered. I'm so sorry. I know how important he was to you. Were you able to tell him everything? Say everything you wanted to say?"

Nodding, I said, "I think so." Then smiling I added, "I got to tell him we're related. He whooped."

"Whooped?"

"Yup. He whooped."

My dear, sweet Henry. Our time together had been brief, but how extraordinary that we'd even met. Knowing that his dearest Sarah had called him home, made the loss more bearable. I'd helped him find his answers and he was able to put his grief to rest. Looking back, I realized he'd done the same for me.

Niko lifted me to my feet. I put my arms around him and buried my head in his chest. "You smell like spice. Like cinnamon. Did you cook after I left?" I looked up at him.

"Yes, my love." He smiled.

"Well, you smell delicious. You are delicious. Maybe that's what we should name the restaurant...Delicious." I held his hand as we walked the brick path between the stones.

Niko laughed. "Absolutely. And the tagline can be, 'A Fusion of Flavors.'"

"Nooooooo. Anything but that."

Epilogue

We opened Olive on Valentine's Day the following year. Two nights prior, we'd had the traditional "friends and family night" to give the kitchen and staff a trial run, and experience our newly hired crew in action. We knew our peeps, especially those in the industry, would give us honest feedback.

Everyone was there—Paris, Rafael, Livia and the Walrus, Wick, heck, half of Grace O'Malley's, Leisa from the Station, Amy from the coffee shop, and Jen from Biblion. After he'd sent out the last dessert of the night, a chocolate pistachio crème brulee, Niko came into the dining room and tapped a knife against a glass. He looked exceptionally handsome in his white chef coat with *Olive* embroidered on it.

"Thank you everyone for being here. We're so happy to share our food, but especially *this moment*, with our family and friends." While he was speaking, servers quietly set a flute of champagne in front of everyone. "Here's to our new adventure and the people we love." He tipped his glass in my direction, and I responded in kind. It was so surreal, seeing the faces of everyone I cared about, all in one place. *Our* place. Tucked into a charming old building in a city that I adored.

The kitchen had stepped out to hear and acknowledge the applause that thundered from the room. "I'd especially like to thank the love of my life." As he said this, Niko walked towards me. "She's been the most brilliant and delightful partner a man could hope for. An unexpected and delicious gift." He emphasized *delicious* as he took my hands in his and kissed them. It made both the room and me laugh. "And with your permission" —he glanced at the table where Livia and Paris sat, then knelt on one knee— "I would ask that you, Genevieve Stewart, do me the honor of becoming my wife?"

The whole world paused for just a beat. Ella Fitzgerald sang softly in the background. Candlelight lit the faces of my nearest and dearest. Hints of chocolate and cinnamon teased the air. Niko held out a velvety dark blue box with a stunning emerald cut diamond inside. My chef Bourbon, with his ridiculous lashes, stared up at me with such love, I felt I could die of happiness.

I nodded. Then nodded again. And finally managed to speak: "Yes," I said, throwing my arms around him. He kissed me passionately and swung me around as people rushed forward to congratulate us. I pictured Henry near the window, his face lit with joy, saying, "Well done, Miss Vie, well done."

I was happy. Truly happy. I knew my Dad would be proud, which made my heart swell. I had finally acknowledged and embraced the things I loved. And Paris was beside himself planning our fall wedding.

From Olive's windows I can see Grace O'Malley's and St. Peter's church, the cemetery where Emily Jane came to rest and where Henry and I said our last goodbye.

Henry. Had I known I was talking to a ghost, I'm not sure I would have stayed on that bench. But I'm ever so glad I did.

Acknowledgments

Maribeth Fischer, there aren't enough words in my vocabulary to thank you. Teacher, mentor, sensei, friend—you are an extraordinary being that I am grateful for every day. You created the most wonderful writing environment for all of us who've taken your classes. The Rehoboth Beach Writers Guild, which you founded, is amazing. What a gift you are.

Greer Maneval, artist sublime (thank you for the sketches in my book!), and the best cheerleader on the planet. For believing I could do this, would do this, and laughing and crying with me through all of my drafts. This book would not be here without you.

Jason Griffin, much-loved son and artist extraordinaire! Thank you for my beautiful cover. You inspire me with how fearless you are with your art, with the publishing world, and with life. I'm so proud of you.

Susan Kehoe (of Browseabout Books), for your wisdom, humor, and most amazing vision. Your suggestions were invaluable, and your support is just the best.

My writing community, wow! How lucky am I? Ethan Joella for leading the way and being extraordinarily patient with my never-ending questions. Jenifer Adams-Mitchell for your laughter and honest feedback. Kim Burnett, Judy Wood, Paul Dyer, Jen Epler, Margaret Kirby, Kathleen Martens, and Lynda Schuler for your encouragement and being in the trenches together.

Nancy Sakaduski for your Beach anthologies and marketing savvy. Winning the Reader's Choice Award gave me the courage to keep going. (And I blame the martini for calling you about the edits!)

Megan Rash and Bill Rash for being two of my favorite human beings and the best real estate team on the planet. Thank you for giving me the time to make this happen. Love you guys!

My foodies! Bob Suppies, my partner in crime for exploring local history, and for allowing me to question you about all things restaurant. Paul Cullen and Bob Yesbek for Eating Rehoboth. My peeps at Saketumi: Mike Ragazzo and Emily Gore-Johnson, for all your input on bartending and service. (My own bartending stint was too long ago in a galaxy far, far away.) And Kaitlyn, Dominique, Joan, Alec, Tammy, Donny, Sara, Ling Ling, and everyone else who brings the fun to my "office."

Thank you to Leah McCloskey, of LM Studio, for my delightfully whimsical website. I kept bringing you lame ideas and you kept saying, "Why do you want this boring site? You're not boring!"

To Betty Raymond, the most avid reader who believed in me from the start.

And to Lois Hoffman of the Happy Self-Publisher, thank you for your divine patience, your industry knowledge, and for getting me to the finish line!

To amazing writers like Lauren Grodstein, my super famous Writing Godmother, a true writer's writer. You are so encouraging and unexpected and real and inspiring. Not to mention delightful, warm, honest, and brilliant, in the best possible way.

I loved Emily Henry's advice: "Write what only you can write. Write what you want, regardless of whether you see anyone else doing the same thing. Don't let yourself be caught up in trends (or frightened off by them, for that matter). Write what you are excited about and over time, learn to trust yourself and your vision."

This is my love letter to Lewes, a place I called home for fourteen years. I'm most grateful to the Lewes Historical Society (now Historic Lewes) for all that you do, and for bringing history to life.

About the Author

D. J. (Deb) Griffin is happiest when writing, as it gives her weirdly wonderful imagination a place to roam. She loves encouraging other writers to tell their stories, but fully embraces how frightening yet exciting that can be. Her short story, The History Lesson, published in The Beach House anthology, won the Reader's Choice Award. Since 2007, she's authored The Local Buzz, a monthly newsletter that features everything fun and new at the Delaware Beaches, where she joyfully resides. Deb is both a science fiction and history nerd who wishes that time travel was her superpower. She loves fabulous food, dogs, and adventures both near and far. Deb is an active member of the Rehoboth Beach Writers' Guild and the Women's Fiction Writers Association. You can follow her writing journey at www.debgriffinwrites.com. *Love, Lewes* is her debut novel.

www.ingramcontent.com/pod-product-compliance
Lightning Source LLC
Chambersburg PA
CBHW022109310726
48972CB00007B/1957